Husrō & SHIRIN

Persian Legends in Love

MARYAM TABIBZADEH

Published by DreamBooks
1300 N ST. NW #017
Washington, DC 2017 U.S.A.
www.dreambookpublisher.com
International Standard Book Number 978-0-9794112-3-6

CONTENTS

Acknowledgements...vii
Dedication ix
Characters...xi

Chapter 1   The Poet Tells the Story 1
Chapter 2   One Night of Revelry Leads to Harsh Punishment.....3
Chapter 3   The Dream...6
Chapter 4   The Painting 14
Chapter 5   Shirin Sees the Painting a Second Time 16
Chapter 6   Shirin Sees Parviz's Painting for the Third Time 18
Chapter 7   The Appearances of Shah-Pour................................20
Chapter 8   Shirin's Trip to the Capital City, Tisfoon 27
Chapter 9   Shirin on Her Way...29
Chapter 10   Parviz in the Meadow 31
Chapter 11   Shirin in Parviz's Castle 38
Chapter 12   Parviz in Armenia...41
Chapter 13   Shah-Pour Returns..44
Chapter 14   Shah-Pour on His Way to Tisfoon 47
Chapter 15   Rebel in the Court...51
Chapter 16   Parviz Hears the Devastating News 53
Chapter 17   Parviz Becomes Shah-Hanshah..............................55
Chapter 18   Shirin Returns to Mahin-Bano 58
Chapter 19   Nizami Recounts Parviz's Wars..............................59
Chapter 20   Parviz Reaches the Land of His Lover.....................68
Chapter 21   Mahin-Bano's Advice to Shirin 71

Chapter 22   The King's Merriment....................................75
Chapter 23   Killing the Lion in the Meadow.............................77
Chapter 24   Shirin in Her Loneliness 85
Chapter 25   Shah-Hanshah Husrō-Parviz 92
Chapter 26   The Birth of the Shah-Hanshah's Son 94
Chapter 27   Shah-Pour Visits with Parviz...............................97
Chapter 28   King Parviz Asks Shah-Pour to See Shirin 101
Chapter 29   Shah-Pour in Tisfoon.....................................108
Chapter 30   Farhad Falls in Love..................................... 111
Chapter 31   Farhad's Pain for Shirin's Love 116
Chapter 32   Farhad's Love Story Reaches Shah Parviz 118
Chapter 33   Husrō-Parviz Seeks Advice................................120
Chapter 34   Farhad Starts His Project 127
Chapter 35   Shirin Visits Farhad on the Mountain.....................130
Chapter 36   Husrō-Parviz Hears About Shirin's Visit to Bistoon... 135
Chapter 37   The Bad News Reaches Shirin..............................139
Chapter 38   Husrō-Parviz's Sympathy Letter to Shirin 145
Chapter 39   Queen Maryam Dies 151
Chapter 40   Husrō-Parviz Without Maryam 154
Chapter 41   Shirin's Answer to the King's Demand.....................156
Chapter 42   Shirin's Loneliness and Sadness..........................159
Chapter 43   Parviz Goes to Shirin's Palace........................... 161
Chapter 44   Returning to His Camp....................................169
Chapter 45   The Wedding 172
Chapter 46   Shirin Gives Parviz a Child..............................179
Chapter 47   Problems at Home 184
Chapter 48   The King's Murder.......................................186
Chapter 49   Shirin and the New King.................................189
Chapter 50   Shirin's Last Day..190
Chapter 51   History: The Wish Comes True but Does It Last?... 192

Glossary 197
References 199
About the Author...201

ACKNOWLEDGEMENTS

Many thanks to Fariba Moezi for the beautiful cover design and Jose Pepito Jr for interior design. I also want to thank **Nicole Hartje for working so hard to format and edit this book.**

I'd like to thank my family and friends for all the encouragement and love I received before and while writing this book.

DEDICATION

I dedicate *Husrō* & Shirin to my family, Sheila, Tara, and P. Mahoutchian, whose encouragement and love gave me the courage and inspiration to write.

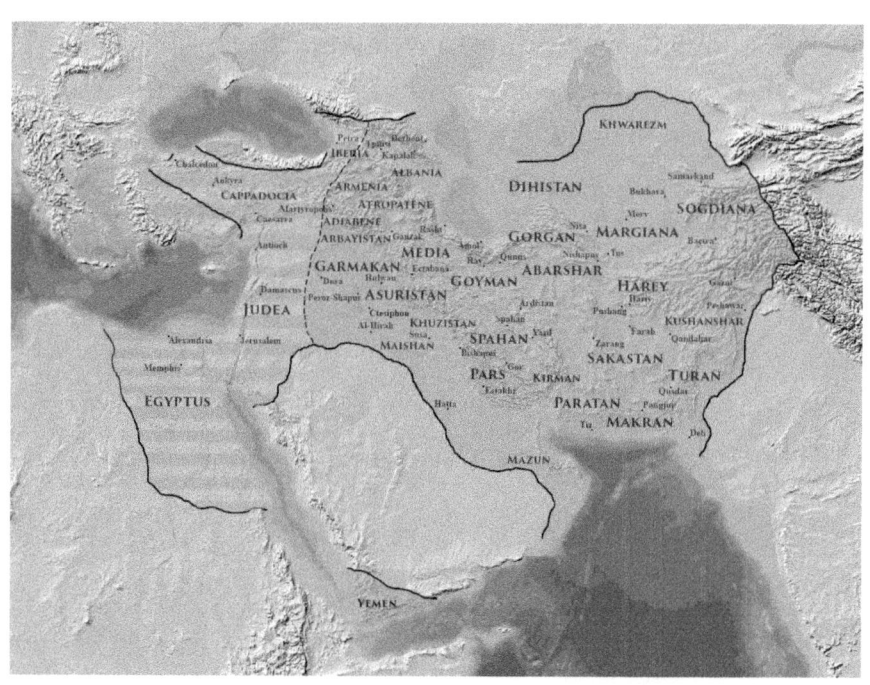

Persian Empire map during the sixth century.

CHARACTERS

Parviz- Crown Prince of the Persian Empire. His name means "ever victorious." Often called Husrō-Parviz.

Shirin- heir to throne of Armenia. Her name means "soft, sweet, surgery, amiable, luscious."

Hormozd- Persian King and father of Parviz

Anoshiravan- Persian King and grandfather of Parviz

Mahin-Bano- Queen of Armenia, Shirin's aunt. Her real name is Shamira.

Shah-Pour- Parviz's man and an artist

Bozorg-Mehr- Parviz's teacher

Bozorg-Omid- Parviz's Prime Minister

Qobād (or Kavadh)- Parviz's son, nicknamed Shiruya

MardanShah- Parviz's son

Shabdiz- A horse black as night

Golgoon- Shirin's horse, reddish in color

Bandooy- Parviz's maternal uncle.

Gostham- Parviz's maternal uncle.

Goordoy- Persian general

Zangoy- Persian general

Farhad- an engineer

Maryam- Princess of Roman Empire, daughter of Caesar

Bahram (or Bahram Choobin)- Persian general

Shahrbaraz- Persian general

Barbed- Parviz's musician

Nakisa- Parviz's harp player

Rostam- Parviz's advisor and champion in Persian stories

Golnoosh, Farangis, Homayoon, Homila, Saman-Khatoon, Mondana- Shirin's friends

Saam- mythical hero in Persian stories

Farshid- aqquaintance of Shah-Pour

Mehrdad- a friend of Parviz

Nizami Ganjavi- Persian author attributed with the original version of *Husrō* & Shirin written in Persian.

CHAPTER 1

○—⊶———⊷—○

The Poet Tells the Story

A ll through the history of Persian poetry, among numerous poets, the name Shirin symbolizes beauty, love, and devotion. But only one tells her life story in detail. So, let us travel back in time and over mountains, seas, and centuries, back to the city of Ganjeh at the house of Nizami Ganjavi in the 12ᵗʰ century and meet the handsome 39-year-old man with a magical voice and flashing eyes. Nizami tells an epic story about love and loss, war, sacrifice, and tragedy. "Shirin," he says, "would not be so famous if it weren't for the Almighty King Parviz." What follows is a the story he toldabout Husrō –Parviz.

○———⌣———○

As a child, Parviz was the sunshine of the court. His sweet smile was so beautiful that it would remind you of the glory of the morning sun. He was so curious about the world, even at five, he couldn't stop looking around and asking questions. His father hired tutors to try and satisfy his questions. He learned so quickly that he mastered reading, writing, and several different languages by the time he was nine. His communication skills were superb, and he could skillfully discuss any subject, from politics to

1

philosophy, with anyone. He won every debate his tutors enrolled him in. At the age of nine, he began learning how to fight. At ten, he could hold his own against thirty-year-old men. He could slay dangerous animals with his sword. With his spear, he could unfasten a knot in the air. With his bow and arrows, he hit targets from one hundred yards away. He caught lions and tigers with his lasso.

When he reached 14, he started to wonder about the existence of right and wrong in the world. He wanted to know more of everything, wanted to gain more knowledge than anyone else.

His father learned of a man named Bozorg-Mehr who was a scholar in the field of science. Bozorg-Mehr understood the hidden knowledge of his time. The King asked him to guide his son.

Bozorg-Mehr was already bent and stooped, with hair and beard white and straggly, by the time he began to tutor Parviz. From the earth to the sky, Saturn, and other stars, the old scholar taught his pupil all he knew about the orbits. He was a sea of knowledge and a master in the conventional arts of his time.

But soon the young student rivaled the teacher in his mastery of knowledge.

"It is time to go into the world," said Bozorg-Mehr. "You can't stay a student forever. Knowledge must be used, or it dies."

CHAPTER 2

One Night of Revelry Leads to Harsh Punishment

After a day of hunting, Parviz came upon a village which was surrounded by new, green pastures. He sat on a hillock overlooking the green valley and started to drink. He was discussing the hunt with his young friends when the night began to spread its black veil over the world.

They rode down into the village, and when curious men came out to greet them, Parviz asked if they might stay overnight. One man invited him to his house, where a small group of men sat around drinking. A musician with the troupe of hunters took out a harp and started to play. Soon people were dancing or drinking and bellowing. Parviz and his friends danced deep into the early morning.

He was unaware that outside his horse was trampling a farmer's land and eating the produce, and that one of the soldiers in their entourage had picked fruits from a tree without permission. However, Shah Hormozd (Parviz's father) had a pact with his people that no one would abuse another. The horses should not mess up anyone's farm, and no person should pick any fruit without the owner's permission.

The next morning as soon as the sun divided night from the day, someone told the Shah what happened the night before. "The Prince," he said, "did not obey your orders. His horse ate from the farm, his soldier took from the tree, and Parviz took over the small home of a poor man where his harp playing kept the man awake."

The Shah got angry and ordered his men to kill Parviz's horse, give his slave to the owner of the orchard, break his harp, and give his throne to the villager at whose house he spent the night.

When the elders came to where Parviz was staying to inform him of the Shah's decision, Parviz thought about what happened and realized that he had been wrong, and his behavior deserved the punishment he received. He asked the elders to take him to his father to ask for forgiveness. The elders went ahead, talked to the King, and asked him to see his son.

The Shah agreed, and Parviz entered the court. He bent his head and said, "Shah-Hanshah, please do not give me more punishment by ignoring me. I am very young, but my guilt is enormous. Please forgive your child's sinful behavior and be dignified. I do not have any problem with all the punishments I've born, but I cannot stand your anger."

All the elders were impressed and moved by his patience. When the Shah saw that his teenaged son was so wise and accepted his punishment with the dignity, he knew the boy was a gift from God. He came down from his throne and kissed his head.

"I am glad that you know what you did was wrong and that you deserved the punishment you received," the Shah said. "As a young Prince, your behavior is critical. If you do not obey the law, who will? And if I do not punish you, how can I punish the others who break the law? You will be in my place one day, and you should learn to be King to the people you are governing. They need to be safe and prosperous if you want our country to be safe and prosperous."

Husrō-Parviz nodded his head in agreement and said, "Good health and long life be upon you. I heard your advice and will remember it as long as I live."

The Shah smiled, then sat his son down beside him. "From now on you are my army commander."

Everyone in the audience cheered and congratulated the Crown Prince.

CHAPTER 3

The Dream

That evening, when the night spread its hair, covering the world in darkness, Parviz went home and recited his prayers. Then he went to bed and fell asleep. In his dream, his grandfather told him, "You will be the sun of the new world. Since you ate sour grapes and did not turn sour, you will find a lover who is sweeter than any woman in the world. Her name is Shirin.

Secondly, they killed your horse, but you did not get mad so you will find a black horse called Shabdiz that is the fastest horse in the universe.

Third: Since Shah gave your throne away, you will gain the throne of the Persian Kingdom.

Fourth: Since you were patient when they broke up your harp, you will find a musician called Barbed whose music will take his audiences to the heavens of imagination. You will find gold in place of stone, four gems in place of four beads."

The Prince woke up with amusement. What kind of dream was that? Is it possible that my grandfather knows what is going to happen to me? Will I really get what he promised? He got up and started walking in his castle looking at the fresh flowers and thinking about his dream but did not know what to make of it. The days that followed, he was occupied by the dream and wondered what it was about and why.

The third morning he woke up early, thinking of the dream. He could not sleep any longer, so he strode down to his garden. The jasmine trees perfumed the air. The sky was blue, and the sun was not yet up. He spotted Shah-Pour, who was sitting on the bench by the fountain with his canvas painting. Shah-Pour was his close acquaintance who was a fantastic artist whose paintings were so beautifully drawn that one would have thought they were alive. Parviz was so happy to see him that early, he started walking faster toward him.

Shah-Pour, who heard his steps, turned toward him and saw the Crown Prince. He jumped up and bowed. "Good morning Your Majesty, I knew you were an early riser, but I've never seen you this early!"

With a chuckle, Parviz answered, "I could not sleep anymore, but I see you are up and working already. What are you painting now?"

"I am trying to paint the sunrise Your Majesty. Do you want to watch?"

"Of course." He sat on the bench next to Shah-Pour.

Shah-Pour started his painting but soon realized that the Crown Prince was in deep thought and didn't say anything about his work. He stopped painting, put his brush aside and asked. "Your Majesty, what is wrong? You are so quiet, I see you deep in your thoughts! What has happened that disturbed my Prince's mind?"

Parviz moved and tilted toward him, gazed into his eyes and said with a chuckle, "You are very observant Shah-Pour; for an artist it is amazing!"

"My Prince if I were not observant I would not be able to draw so precisely but am specifically interested in your well-being and cannot sit still when I see the concern in your face."

"I am not sure if it should be anyone's concern. It was a dream, but for some reason, it is occupying my mind."

Shah-Pour said "My dear Shahzadeh will you share it with me? I have traveled much and have seen wonders in this world. Maybe I can be of some help in the interpretation of your dream."

Husrō-Parviz stood up and started pacing. "A few nights ago I saw my grandfather, the Shah Anoshiravan, who told me four things were in my future. The first was since I lost my throne to the villager, I will gain the throne to the Persian Empire. This dream disturbed me since I love my father and do not want anything to happen to him. That dream repeated last night."

"I hope my King lives a long life and all his years and months are full of happiness. But as long as the world exists, no one will be alive forever, and the King is getting older. You are the Crown Prince, and it is evident that you will have your ancestors' throne sooner or later. But you said there were four things in your future, what are the other three?"

Husrō-Parviz sat down and said, "The others are more absurd than the first. He said, "You will find gold in place of stone, four gems in place of four beads. You ate the sour grape of punishment without getting mad, so you will have a sweet lover called Shirin. For losing your horse, instead, you will get the black horse named Shabdiz and will find the most famous musician of your time whose name is Barbed!""

Shah-Pour clapped his hand and said, "Precisely, they are all true."

Husrō-Parviz shrugged and asked "What are you talking about? What is precise about it?"

He bowed again and said, "Shah of my heart, if you permit me I will tell you a thing about what I know."

Husrō-Parviz patted his shoulder and said, "You don't need permission to talk to me my friend, go ahead and say what is on your mind."

So Shah-Pour told this story. "There on the other side of Caspian Sea, and by the Seven Lakes, is the Armenian land. A woman rules this land which extends from the Aron to Armenia. Nowhere in that land do you see any rotten places. She rules everything and is the Shah of Armenia. She has castles on the tallest mountains, and God only knows how vast her treasury is. She also keeps thousands of livestock in her pastures and countless numbers of poultry. She is not married, but she has more than any man in that country, they call her Mahin-Bano for her being so great."

Husrō-Parviz raised his hand and said: "Yes, I heard of her at a Nowruz party since her gift was very impressive and expensive."

Shah-Pour continued, "Yes, my King she is living a lavish life and is jubilant. Her real name is Shamira. She has palaces for each season. In the spring, she goes to Moghan so she can walk in lush green pastures. In the summer, she settles in the Armenian mountains and travels from pasture to pasture and harvest to harvest. In the fall, she settles in the Abkhaz and starts her hunting trips. And finally, in the winter, she stays in the Barda since Barda has a warmer climate. That is how she lives—in her palaces and with her friends."

Husrō-Parviz interrupted him and asked, "You said my dream is real, but I do not see any relation between her and my dream."

"Your Majesty, if you give me a few minutes I will show you the relationship. The fact is, in this world, Mahin-Bano has only one niece, and that is all. Her niece can brighten anyone's night like the new moonlight. Her eyes are black like the essence of life itself. She is tall and slender; her skin is silvery white. Her teeth are like pearls. Her lips are naturally red like agate, and her braided hair looks like two black snakes. Her mouth seems to have a hundred tongues speaking sweet words. You see so many people attracted to her like butterfliesgathering around a candlelight. Her face is so beautiful that you cannot compare it to any flower or the majesty of sunshine. Her breasts are like two silky pomegranates with beautiful flowers on the top. Her neck is prettier than a deer's, and so are her eyes.

"People dream about her, but nobody has found her sunshine face at night. Men are dying to see the arch of her eyebrows. In her hand, there are ten fingers like pens seeming to give killing orders to those wishing to gain her love. I was told that she has thousands of suitors. Her name is Shirin. People call her lips nectar, and they think she is Mahin Bono's Crown Princess. The beautiful ladies who are the commanders of that land all obey her. From beautiful noblewomen, she has forty girls whose beauties can calm your soul. They each play the harp, and they go with her from one place to another. They are single, and they have nothing to do but have fun. If you have heard of heaven, then that place is heaven and those ladies its virgins.

"But when it is time for fighting, they take from lions their claws and from elephants their tusks. Shirin also has a horse in her stable which can quickly win any race. That horse runs mountains like she has iron legs. She is just as fast when going through water in the sea. This Shabrang is called Shabdiz. Shirin is in love with that bird of the night. She has a chain made of gold which fastens to Shabdiz's legs. I have never seen anyone sweeter than Shirin, nor any black horse like Shabdiz."

Husrō-Parviz, who was drawn to the story clapped his hands and said, "Bravo Shah-Pour. I thought your art was only in painting, but now I see you are a master of storytelling, too. Tell me please, that this was only a story you just made up."

"Your Majesty, what I told you is not a story. There is truth in every word I said,"

"You are not telling me my grandfather actually promised me this beautiful Armenian Princess and her horse?"

"Your Majesty that is what I am telling you. If there is one woman in this world who is worthy of you that is Shirin, and I think Your Majesty deserves Shabdiz as his horse.

"Seeing is believing my friend. You are a real artist. Draw me their pictures and let me see if she is as beautiful as you describe her."

Smiling he patted Shah-Pour's shoulder, and then got up and left. However, his mind now was fuller than before, and excitement ran through every part of his body. The young Prince was experiencing a feeling that he never had before. When Shah-Pour told this story, everything else flew from Parviz's mind, and love awakened. From that day on, Parviz was so disturbed that he could not sleep without thinking of the girl in the story. Every day he thought about the story and his dream.

A few days passed, and he was happy with what he heard until Shah-Pour arrived.

"Long live my Prince. The painting that you ordered is ready. Do you want to see it?"

Parviz felt his heartbeat increase. "Yes, of course, I want to see it." When he held the portrait, his hands shook, and he sat down to overcome his emotion. He looked at the painting. It was a beautiful picture, so natural that he felt the girl was looking right at him. He wanted to talk to her.

Shah-Pour saw his shaking hands, and his admiration for the painting and said, "What are you thinking now Your Majesty? Is she beautiful?"

"Oh, my dear friend, she is more beautiful than what I imagined, but your story has robbed me of any rest. I have had a problem sleeping since I was wondering about the girl you described to me so vividly that I fell in love with her without seeing her. Since you build such a good story, you need to finish."

Shah-Pour bowed and said "I do not doubt that you would like to have her, since no one can measure up to her beauties and talent. She assuredly is the best Queen for our future King."

"Ok, my friend let's not go too far. We know she is perfect, but is she unattached? You say so many are in love with her, what if she has someone in her mind? What if she is in love with someone else?"

"My King, there is always a possibility, but although she is tall and beautiful like a mature flower, she is too young to be in love since she is only a teenager. She was trained to become Queen of Armenia, that is why she is so smart and talented. But she's only a bud just opening up. I am sure she will fall in love with you if you want her to."

The Prince's heart started to beat harder again, and a broad smile covered his face. "Then you need to be sure of this; I want you to go to her and see what she is doing and who she is seeing. If she does not have anyone in her heart, then see if you can make her love me. You must see if her heart is like wax or if it is made of iron and wants nothing to do with me. Then come back and tell me."

Shah-Pour said, "Oh my King, I wish you to be happy and to be loved by everyone. You should know that when I start painting, people can only bow to its beauty. Do not get upset since it does no good to have pain in your heart. You should be happy and not worry since I will do everything possible. I will borrow the art of running from zebras and flying from birds and I will not rest until I see her. I will not sleep and will not come until I bring her love to you. I will take her out of her house just like the fire that takes the soft iron from the stone or the power that makes the gem hiding inside a rock. I will work with anyone either flower or a thorn, and if I am lucky, I will make her fall in love with you. If I see that I am not able to persuade her, then I will let my King know."

"That is an excellent idea. I will be waiting to hear about your trip and your marvelous work."

Shah-Pour bowed and left the court leaving Parviz drowning in his thoughts.

He ran his horse in the deserts and mountains. He worked hard to get to Armenia as soon as he could. Riding a horse under sunshine in the early spring was not easy, but he had a goal that was dear to him.

He crossed the desert of the south and ran toward the mountains of the north. He finally arrived in the Armenian mountains where Shirin and her friends were living. When he arrived, the grass was new, and as far as he could see, there were tulips all over the land. The blue stones reflected red and yellow from the abundance of blooms, and from top of each mountain, all one could see was the color of emerald with beautiful flowers everywhere.

There was an old convent in a cave with an elderly head priest who opened his convent to any passersby without a place. Shah-Pour stopped at this convent and there he rested since he was overly tired from his long ride. When night combed its hair and the day's light died, Shah-Pour asked the priests if they knew where Shirin and her friends would be the next morning.

One priest told him, "Beyond this big rock there is a beautiful valley full of flowers and waterfalls. Every day, Princess Shirin and her friends, who are early risers, go there."

Shah-Pour painted Parviz's face and went to bed.

CHAPTER 4

The Painting

The next morning before the sun woke from her night's sleep and before the beautiful ladies went to their heavenly place, Shah-Pour went to the valley full of flowers. There he placed the painting in the trunk of a tree. Then he disappeared and waited for the beautiful ladies to arrive at the green pasture. They arrived and happily started cutting flowers to make bouquets. They splashed the petals around with laughter and joy. They were brides without grooms. They brought wine and started drinking while they added flowers to their flowers. Then they started dancing and singing, running from one blossoming bush to another.

Princess Shirin, amidst all those sweet faces, was like a moon among the stars. She had a pleasant time with her friends, sometimes pouring wine and sometimes drinking herself. At one point, when she was running from a flowering tree to another, she saw the painting.

She told the girls, "Please bring me that picture and tell me, who painted it?" They brought the picture and told her that they did not know whose face was in the painting or who the painter was. She stared at it for a long time. She could not take her eyes

14

of the picture. She would become drunk by looking at it so she drank more wine.

Her friends hid the painting, but she asked for it again and again. The guards were worried that she had fallen in love with the art, so they tore that beautiful picture to pieces, and when Shirin asked for it, they said that demons had placed it in the tree and they should leave the place at once. The group left that pasture and went to another field.

CHAPTER 5

Shirin Sees the Painting a Second Time

When the day brought the color of light, Shah-Pour followed the beauties without them noticing. Like a shadow, he went wherever they did. He painted another picture and placed it against another flowering tree.

The girls got to that pasture and started playing. While dancing on the new grass, Shirin saw the painting again in a tree. Her heart started flying like a bird, and her tongue could not say a word. She thought she was dreaming and asked her friend, "Can you see the painting?"

Her friend pretended that she could not see anything, and while she was trying to convince her that there was no painting, another girl took the picture and hid it. Her friend told the Princess, "It was the work of fairies. They play lots of tricks as you know." Then, they left that place too.

That night, they stayed in another pasture, played music and danced. Soon the day came out of night's skirt, and the sun's golden crown spread its rays over the world once again. They began walking in the midst of the beautiful scenery. The ground was green like an emerald and the weather was as sweet as the love for a child. The breeze blew like the wind of heaven.

The anemones made their home amidst the stones and the winds combed the grass's hair. They could hear the sound of nightingales and other singing birds everywhere. The birds were playing beak to beak and in every direction, one could see them playing with joy amongst the flowers.

CHAPTER 6:

Shirin Sees Parviz's Painting for the Third Time

The painter hurried to their place and painted another painting as he had before. Princess Shirin was playing when she spotted the painting she loved so much. She began to wonder about being tricked so she stopped and went and took the painting. In its reflection, she saw herself and became unconsciously out of time and place.

Shirin was furious and told her companion, "You tricked me and made me think it was a fairy's trick, and there was not a real picture. But this painting is real, and I have it in my hand. Did you destroy the other two paintings?"

When the beauties found that the most beautiful Princess was sad, they realized that it was not the work of fairies and it was not something to forget quickly. They regretted tearing the paintings and began saying how beautiful the third painting was. When Shirin realized that they were telling the truth, she decided to ask them to help her find the person whose face was on the painting.

They stated that they would try to find out who the painting belonged to and whose face was painted on the paper. She told them, "I cannot hide it from you since you are my best friends and I like to share my feelings. I am so much in love with this painting; I was sorrowful when I lost it, the first time. When I saw the painting the second time, all my being was happy and I wanted to hold it. But when it disappeared I thought I was going crazy. I thought there was no painting except in my imagination."

"Well we did not know that you were so much in love with the picture, and we honestly thought it was a trick made by fairies," one maid said.

"Now that we know, we will help you in any way we can to find the man this picture belongs to," said another girl.

Shirin said, "Let's not hide our feeling, we can drink in front of this sweet picture." So, they started drinking and singing love songs. The beauties' beloved icon held a cup of bitter wine and became drunk on its bitterness and the sweet aroma of love. Each time she sipped the wine she kissed the painting. When she became drunk, her fever rose higher. She told one of the maids, "Go sit by the road and ask anyone who is passing about this man whose face is in this fascinating painting."

The girl obeyed but the more she asked, the less she found. Nobody knew the man. Shirin was getting impatient and wanted to know the identity of the man that she was falling in love with by just looking at his picture. Sadness crept all over her when she imagined it was no one in the world but the painter's imagination.

In the 5th century, the small country of Persian Armenia was one of many countries in the Persian Empire. Although Shirin's aunt was the Shah of Armenia and Hormozd was the Shah-Hanshah of Persia, no one had ever seen the Crown Prince Parviz, so none knew the face in the painting.

CHAPTER 7

The Appearances of Shah-Pour

A few days passed before Shah-Pour decided to show himself to the Princess of beauty. When Shirin saw him, she found some resemblance to the painting, so she told her companion, "Call that Persian man and ask him about the picture. He might know something about it and recognize who is in the painting." The companion went to Shah-Pour and asked him:

"Hello stranger, where are you from?"

"I come from a faraway land where our Shah-Hanshah lives, the capital city of the Persian Empire."

"We have a puzzle that no one can solve in this area and thought you might be able to solve it."

Shah-Pour smiled and said, "For your beautiful face I will obey, if I can."

"We have found a painting which shows a handsome man and our lady wants to know who he is and what is his faith."

"Oh, my beautiful fairy, this is a gem that cannot efficiently be priced, even if I could, I cannot do it here." He smiled and walked away.

The companion went to Shirin and told her." That man is very mysterious, he did not say he didn't know but said this is a gem that cannot be priced!"

When Shirin heard this, her blood pressure raised and she said, "I think he knows, please ask him to come here and we will see."

The companion went to where Shah-Pour was sitting and said, "My Lady wishes to talk to you. Can you come and be our guest?"

Shah-Pour smiled while standing up and said, "Oh, of course. Who can refuse such a kind invitation from a beautiful fairy like you?"

The girl blushed and said, "Let's go then and stop talking like this, I am inviting you because our Princess wants to speak to you."

"Still, I will be walking with you to see her. I cannot refuse that either. We admire beautiful flowers and stop to see their beauties; it is the same with people. I cannot stop myself from admiring the beauty of a young girl like you. It is my honor to walk with such a beautiful lady."

The girl was amused by his tongue and his openness, but he was a stranger, so she said." That is ok. I just want to tell you that I usually do not trust the strangers and do not believe their sweet songs."

"That is very smart of you. However, my compliment is the truth, and it is not for you to be scared. I ask nothing from you."

"Well, we are there now. The lady in green is the Princess. Go ahead and introduce yourself."

Shah-Pour saw her tall body, her black hair spreading on her marble shoulders; her lips were like a hundred pounds of sugar and her eyes were full of naz (coquetery). Upon seeing such a beautiful work of art, the painter's tongue could not talk. Instead, he bowed.

She called him. "You, the stranger in this land, do not be strange any longer. Let's be friends for a few minutes."

That clever man heard her voice and decided to be quiet for a while. That man had but one tongue, and that one was fastened by his admiration of her beauty, so he said, "Long live the most beautiful lady! Are you a woman or a fairy?"

Shirin laughed and asked him to sit. Then she asked him, "We have a puzzle, can you solve it for us?"

The man answered her. "I have seen good and bad everywhere. But my God never covers any secret from me. From west to east I have traveled from country to country. Do not worry about the land because I know everything from the sky to the earth; you can ask me anything you wish."

When Shirin found that the man was a boaster, she said, "In that case, what do you know about this painting?"

In answer, Shah-Pour the painter said, "I hope no bad comes your way, my beautiful lady. The story of his face is long, and I have a secret from this man. I will tell you all if I can speak to you alone."

Shirin asked her companions to disappear. When they were alone, he started to talk. "This handsome man is the sunshine of seven countries. He is like Alexander the Great and Darius the Great and is a reminder of them. He is so attractive that we call him the God of Beauty. He is Shah-Hanshah Parviz, who is the Crown Prince of the Persian Empire." Shirin was listening to this sweet talk, asking herself, *What is he like? Does he have someone he likes?*

He said, "I do not know why you are hiding your feelings. If you are looking for a cure, you cannot hide your pain from your doctor."

Shirin got angry, but her anger made her much prettier. However, she was in love and wanted to know more about this man she loved without seeing. She heard so much from the stranger and the more she heard, the more she fell in love. *Oh, isn't this beautiful* she imagined, *being the Queen of Persia and having the man of my dreams as my husband?*

She sat by the stranger and said, "Please give me advice and tell me what I have to do? My heart is in pain. I am so much in love with this picture that it seems I am worshipping this image day and night. Please help me, and I am sure I will be able to help you someday too. Now that I told you my secret you should tell me what you know."

The magician could not say anything but the truth. He fell and knelt in front of her. "Oh you the best of best, you deserve to be on the throne and be the honor of Kings. Swear to the person I am debted to; I will tell you the truth since you were truthful with me. I am the person who drew Parviz's face in this painting. Any painting that the painter draws has a face, but it does not have spirit. I learned how to draw, but someone else makes life possible. If you are in love with his face then think about how you will feel if you see him in person? You will see the world full of light. He is an excellent man who is very brave and fast. With love, he is gentle like a deer but with his enemy, he is fierce like a lion. He is a flower without the winds of the fall. He is a branch of youth in spring; he is still very young like the new growth of a boxwood. He is like a sky without any clouds. When he works with his sword, he can easily kill a lion. He is so rich that when he gives, you will see a mile of camels. He bests everyone when it comes to swordplay. And although his face is as handsome as a new spring, it is his thought and artful work which make him so beautiful. With all the good luck he has, day and night he is thinking about you."

Shirin was surprised. "He thinks of me? How? Where did he hear about me?"

"He saw you one night in his dreams, and from then on he lost his wisdom and his consciousness. He does not drink and has no fun with anyone. Neither can he sleep at night or rest during the day. He does not want anyone but sweet Shirin. This kind of bitterness is unbearable to anyone. That is why he sent me to you, and I am here. I told you everything; good or bad, you can decide."

Shirin was listening to him like she was drinking surgery water. She almost fell multiple times but tried to stay in place. She realized that the picture she liked so much was an image of a real person who was going to be the King of Kings. The magician's words transfixed her. He had described the face in the painting as a lovely young man with all the criteria that the Prince of Persia should have.

If that was not enough, he told that this extraordinary young man was madly in love with her although he had never laid an eye on her! She was raised as a Princess and was trained to resist her emotion and think clearly, but she was just like any teenager rife with troubling hormones.

That day passed, and Shah-Pour left to go back to the convent. She could not sleep that night. She wanted the night to grow short and bring the sunshine so she could go back to the pasture and talk to the Persian who was her messenger of love. She trusted him more than anyone else. The night finally passed, and it became day. She asked her companions to ride toward the pasture near the convent. They had to travel a long distance, but she had ridden horses since her childhood.

They passed the green fields one after another until they got to the pasture near the convent. They spread a beautiful woven carpet under a willow tree and put out cushions for their Princess to sit on. The scenery was breathtaking. The sky was bright blue with no clouds. The green pasture was full of flowering trees with thousands of daffodils like golden rings on the ground.

She had just sat down on the cushion when she spotted Shah-Pour coming toward her. Her heart beat in her chest so crazy that she was afraid her companions would know her secret. She told them, "Look at the daffodils all over, can you each bring me a bouquet? I will give a real prize for the biggest and best ones."

The girls scattered all over the pasture each wanting the title. Shirin's own prize was to talk to her messenger of love. She was eager to ask him what to do next. Shah-Pour came close and bowed to her.

"Long live Your Majesty the Princess of Armenia, all is good I hope?"

"Hello Shah-Pour, I am fine. Come and sit here I would like to talk to you more."

"I am sure you would like to hear more about our brave Prince. Am I right?"

"Yes, your words about your painting did not let me sleep last night. I was wondering what we should do now, what is the next step to take?"

Shah-Pour, who was excited and saw that his magic had been working decided to take her to his master instead of telling him that she was interested. So, he said, "I think you should not mention any of our conversation to anyone. You can take a hunting trip with Shabdiz, but from there change your direction and run out of the hunting area toward the capital city of Persia. As I understand it, nobody can get close to you or catch up when you're on Shabdiz." Then he looked into Shirin's eyes and took a very expensive ring out of his pocket and gave it to her.

"This is his ring, if, on your way, you see the new King, show him this ring. You will see his horse wearing gold horseshoes. His clothes are covered with jewelry. His belt and his hat are covered with rubies, and his face looks much more handsome than his jewels. If you reach the capital, ask for his palace and go there. Show his ring to the servants, and they will welcome you. He will see you if he is in town. I will follow you as soon as I can and will take you to him. This ring is a precaution for any unexpected problems that might arise."

The girls came back with their laughter and their bouquets of flowers. Shah-Pour grew quiet and said goodbye soon after. Shirin looked at the flowers they brought for her and started her judging. The game was based on arrangement and the kind of flowers picked. Some were fragrant, and some were not.

Shirin seemed calm and relaxed during the process, but inside she was in turmoil. Should she listen to the strange Persian man and run away? Would she be captured? What would her aunt do? Would her aunt hate her if she came back? Like all teenagers, she saw herself capable of making hard decisions, and she did not want her companions or her aunt to stop her from doing what she was about to do. The Crown Prince was in love with her, and she wanted to see him as soon as possible. She would be the future Queen of the Persian Empire, and when she achieved that goal, her aunt would be proud of her.

Mondana, her best friend, won the prize. Once the winner was chosen, she asked everyone to pack and go back home. Talking and joking, they all packed up and went to the palace.

It took Shirin several days before she decided to run away. She decided on a night when the world covered like black smoke and her eyes were sleepy. Shirin went to her aunt Mahin-Bano and said, "My dear aunt, I'd like to go hunting tomorrow. Will you let me have Shabdiz? I would like to ride him on my hunt. I will come back. I might be able to shoot a few birds or a deer too."

Mahin-Bano said, "Oh my dear beautiful moon, instead of a horse ask me for one hundred properties. This black horse Shabdiz rumbles like thunder and is as fast as the wind. I do not want him to hurt you. But if you insist on riding him, you need to be very careful and make him obey your orders."

Shirin's face opened up like a rose petal. She thanked her aunt and went to bed ecstatic.

CHAPTER 8

Shirin's Trip to the Capital City, Tisfoon

When the sun came out of the night's womb, and its golden rays spread around the city. Shirin told her companions, "We are going to the wilderness to hunt, make ready to leave as soon as possible."

They all bowed and said, "Your wish is our command, we will get prepared for the trip." They packed and changed their clothes to look like male servants (the fashionable outfit for riding and hunting). They circled Shirin, and when she mounted her horse, they did the same.

They rode toward an emerald green pasture, and from there to other pastures equally lush. Shirin pushed Shabdiz and soon pulled far ahead of her friends. They thought that her horse had taken off with her. They did not know this was her plan.

They followed her for a long time, but like chasing their shadows, they never were able to reach her. They searched right and left until darkness, and finally, they went back home. They were away from their Shah and were sad and unhappy. Arriving late at night, they went to see Mahin-Bano and told her what had happened.

She was devastated by the news, she stepped down from her throne and sat on the floor crying hard. She moaned for Shirin and her brother saying, "Oh my beautiful niece. I guess the evil eyes has stolen you from me. You were my flower, but the wind took you away and threw you somewhere I do not know. What happened? You don't love us anymore? You are like a deer who became tired of gazelles but will be captured by a lion. You were my cypress whose branches were like veins in my body. Your face was the sunshine; who is it shining on now? I have lost it. Who is going to find it?" She cried all night until dawn when she finally fell asleep.

In her sleep, she dreamt that she had a hawk who flew out of her hand. She became so upset wondering why the bird flew away, but then, the hawk came back and sat on her hand. When the sun came out of night's well, army officers came to her and said, "If you order us, we will go after her and find her wherever she has gone."

Mahin-Bano looked at the officer and thought about it. She felt better after her dream. She had a hope that she did not want to shatter. She hoped that like the hawk in her dream Shirin would be back someday, and she did not wish to smash this dream with a reality which scared her to death. *What if she was thrown off by the horse and is dead? What if a lion has torn her apart and her officers find only her clothing?* So she replied, "Thank you for the offer, but even if we became the sky and could see all places we wouldn't even see the dust from Shabdiz. It is useless to go after a bird who flew away. If a dove flies away, do not cry since it will come back if it is alive."

When the officers heard her answer, they could do nothing but obey her wishes.

CHAPTER 9

Shirin on Her Way

Shirin and Shabdiz rode fast toward Parviz and the place she thought her love was living. The road was long and arduous in some locations and she had to ride the horse for six hundred miles. She carried with her some food, some water, a cotton mattress, and a tent.

She avoided all human contact in case her aunt's army had been ordered to follow her. When she got out of Armenian territory and entered Azerbaijan, she sought out villages to rest and find food. She was wearing male servant's clothing, so no one knew she was a girl traveling alone. Still, she was extra cautious going from village to village. She did not stay in one place too long except to rest and eat. She would ask directions and ride on. She was dusty from riding in the mountains and valleys for fourteen days. Shabdiz was like a commando who was as fast as the wind and she was able to spend a few nights at convents along the way.

One morning, the black color of the evening became disappointed and Shirin started her horse toward another city. She rode into a prairie which was as breathtaking as heaven. There was a mountain covered with grass and thousands of wildflowers dancing under the sun. In the middle of that meadow was a pond made of fresh, clear spring water. She was tired of riding this long trip. Dust covered her from head to toe. The weather had been getting hotter as she moved south, so the water was inviting.

She needed to know if anybody was around before jumping in the water, though. She kicked her horse and circled the pond but found no one around. She looked on all sides and did not see any dwelling in sight.

She dismounted her horse and fastened it to a tree. Then she took off her clothes and jumped into the water. It felt so good to get in and wash off the dust after several days of no bathing. She swam slowly in the coolness. The blue water covered her body so that she looked like a moon shining in the night sky. Her hair spread out in the water, and she washed it as if she expected there would be a dear guest arriving.

CHAPTER 10

Parviz in the Meadow

After Parviz had sent Shah-Pour, he waited days and nights to hear from Armanestan, hoping to see his lover. He spent his days with Shah-Hanshah or went hunting. The Shah-Hanshah loved him and called him "My Crown Prince."

He was the King's love until the evil eyes changed everything. Shah-Hanshah had an enemy called Bahram. Bahram decided to create a split between the King and his brave Crown Prince to weaken both of them and become King himself. To achieve this goal, he decided to make coins in the name of the Crown Prince and spread them around the town; he thought it would make Shah-Hanshah suspicious of the Crown Prince and willing to kill or imprison him. Once that happened it would be easy for Bahram to defeat the old King.

He also wrote a letter to Shah-Hanshah stating, "Now that the Prince Parviz wishes to become King I will support him with all my power to overthrow you and give him the Kingdom."

His trick worked. When Shah-Hanshah, became aware of the coins spreading everywhere bearing the name of the Crown Prince, he became sad and angry. It was customary that the coins had only the name of the King. Seeing coins with the name of Parviz meant only one thing; that he was getting ready to steal the crown. He knew that people loved his son, and he knew of the Crown Prince's capabilities. Shah-Hanshah wondered, *What can I do to stop him? Is he going to kill me? Capture me?* He started drinking and told the informant to leave him alone. Then he asked his prime minister, "You have heard the disturbing news about my son, what do you think we should do?"

The prime minister, who was fond of Parviz, said, "Long live the King. If indeed he ordered such a thing, there is no harm in it. He will be the King sooner or later. He is your Crown Prince. What harm is there if you say it was your idea for people to have coins with the Crown Prince's name on it?"

"Oh, you are getting old and are not as smart as you used to be. There was no harm done if I decided to have my son's name on the coins. But he did it behind my back and without any consultation with me which means one thing—he has a plan. He wants to either kill me or imprison me. I need to act faster than him. I do not mind him becoming the new King, but I am angered by his ungratefulness. I loved him and gave him everything he needed and now that he is a young lion wanting to make me an old wolf! I will put him in prison so everyone knows that it is not right to repay kindness with treason."

"Long live Shah-Hanshah, are you sure you can do such a thing? You are talking about a brave Crown Prince who you so loved. He is your son, not anyone else's. If you decide in a hurry, you might regret your decision. Please sleep on this and decide tomorrow when you are calm. If you still feel this way tomorrow morning, do what you choose."

Shah-Hanshah accepted his pleas and decided to trap the Crown Prince the next morning. However, Bozorg-Mehr heard the story and went to Parviz's palace. The Crown Prince had just come back from hunting, and when he saw his teacher, he dismounted his horse with respect and went toward the older man. "Dorood (hello) to my great teacher who taught me all I know. What brings you here?"

"Long live Shahzadeh (Crown Prince or the Prince) I need to talk to you in private, please tell your men to stay here for a few minutes so I can tell you important news."

Husrō-Parviz told his companions, "Please stay here; I will be back as soon as I can." He guided his old teacher toward his room. Once inside he offered him a chair and sat next to him.

"Bozorg-Mehr, I see you are very disturbed, what has happened? Can I help solve your problem?"

"My King you have been the smartest student I had ever had, yes I am disturbed. I am afraid for your life and want you to depart the capital as soon as possible."

Husrō-Parviz leaned toward the old teacher looked into his wrinkled face and with an astonishing voice said "What? You are afraid for my life! What has happened? Can you be more specific?"

Bozorg-Mehr put both of his hands together on his chest and bent down his head. "Your father is furious with you and wants to harm you. I suggest that you go away for a while until his anger subsides."

Husrō-Parviz got up and started pacing the room. "But why? He is my father and loves me. What have I done to cause such anger?"

"You do not know why?"

"No, of course, I do not, I am in his service day and night why should he be mad at me?"

Bozorg-Mehr wriggled in his chair, but managed to calm himself and cleared his throat and said, "You know that when a new King gets his Kingship, there is a custom to mint coins in the name of the new Shah?"

The Shahzadeh stopped and said with a frown, "Yes of course."

"Well someone has been minting coins in your name in several satrapies of Iran, and the informers brought the new coins to your father."

The Prince stopped and sat on the chair. "Obviously, it was done without the knowledge of my father otherwise; he would not get upset."

"Yes, my King, that is true. He thinks you have done it and spread the coins to gain support from people while setting up a revolt against him."

"But I have not done it, and I had no idea of the event; how can this be possible?"

The old man shook his head and said, "Well one possibility is that someone is trying to create a divide between you and your father."

"Who can it be?"

"There are so many who do not like your father's particular way of governing, and they are well aware of your popularity among the people. If Shah-Hanshah kills you, then it is very easy to take him off the throne."

"In that case, if I run away he will think I am guilty of all charges and will never want to see me. I want to go and tell him that he is mistaken and I did not do it."

"You know your father and how anger blinds him. If you go near him, you will be arrested or even killed. I tell you my King; the best way to temper his anger is for you to be away for a while. Go somewhere you like, be away from the capital and have fun and please do it fast. Tonight is the best time."

Husrō-Parviz looked around the room, and his gaze froze on the old man's face. His teacher's eyes were begging him, and his worried face was contagious. He felt a fear he had never felt in his life, so said in a warm voice, "My dear teacher, I will accept your recommendation and I thank you for your concerns."

Bozorg-Mehr got up, bowed and said, "Long live my King. Go and have fun. I am sure everything will be ok soon, and you can come back happily. I will let God guide you now and take my leave."

Husrō-Parviz got up and hugged his teacher goodbye. Then he went to his housekeepers. He told them, "I am taking a week or two for a hunting trip. You can enjoy yourself while I am gone. If a lady who is as beautiful as a peacock and rides a horse black like a crow comes to this castle, please bring her in since she is my dearest guest. Make her welcome and serve her like a Queen. If she does not want to stay in this castle for any reason, please find a castle where she likes and help her be happy."

He then said goodbye. He took his men and, like the wind, ran out of the capital. He decided then and there to go toward Armenia where his beloved lived. He was sad and worried about the King's anger and tried to run as fast as he could. Man and horse only stopped once where they should have stopped twice. Later that day, the horses grew tired in the same place where Shirin was bathing. Parviz ordered his men to stop and give food to the animals. He alone meandered around the magnificent scenery. A tall mountain covered with wildflowers, green pastures, and a pond in the middle. He strolled around the hollow while thinking, *Is it possible for me to get both Shirin and Shabdiz? Really!*

He was not aware that that black horse and his beautiful beloved were close by. He continued looking around, the water was impossibly clear but what was inside took his breath away. He saw a beautiful lady swimming in the pond like the prettiest spring blossom.

Her body was like a snowy mountain beneath the water. She

stood, and Parviz looked at her beautiful breasts, watched her combing her long black hair back behind her ears.

The Prince's heart flared seeing the naked woman. She was unaware of his stare and when she got out of the water she saw him, a tall, handsome man mounted on a horse. She was disturbed and did not have any other way to cover herself except by pulling her hair over her naked body.

Parviz's heart begged him to look more, to get closer to that beautiful being. But he saw her discomfort and, putting aside his lustful thoughts, decided to look the other way. His heart was melting inside, with the fire of lust like gold mixed with silver in flames. He kept his eyes looking away. He waited. He was a nobleman and did not want to shame a lady. He looked up the mountain so she could cover herself. Shirin ran toward her clothes, dressed fast, and mounted Shabdiz.

She told herself, *Oh this gentleman who was standing on the other side of the pond was so much like my lover. How come I am under his spell if he is not my lover? I heard that he wears rubies on his hat and his belt. If it was him then why I did not see any rubies? He was wearing peasant's clothing.* She did not know that Kings changed their attire for fear of enemies.

Her heart was begging her to go back to the gentleman. He was a real person. But her brain told her to continue on her way. "It is not good to pray for two Gods; you cannot worship two Gods at the same time. Even if this young man is my King, it is better to meet him properly." So, she snapped the reins of her horse and galloped off like a wind swishing away.

When Parviz thought the girl was done getting dressed, he looked back. He saw no one around the pond. He rode his horse around the lake and saw nothing, only the wind whisking through the trees, and his reflection on the lake's surface. He dismounted his horse and started looking around. *How did she disappear?* He looked up at the trees thinking that maybe she had become a bird and flown away. Then he sat down and looked at the water, hoping to see her beneath the surface like a fish.

He told himself, "I found a spring but did not enjoy it. I saw the river but did not wet my lips. I had a jewel in my grip but released it. I saw a flower in the morning but did not pick it. A beautiful blossom came out of the pond, but I don't know if it was a dream or reality. Now, I see nothing. Who told me to turn my head when luck was with me? Which monster said to leave heaven? It is good to be patient but one must remember the wise Indian prophet's saying: *When you find food, hurry up and eat it fast.* In this orchard with all these yellow and red flowers the person who picks them does not get disappointed. Now my heart fills with sadness."

He looked around. *How could she disappear so fast? She couldn't be a fairy because fairies couldn't hide in the water. It wouldn't be good for the Crown Prince to fall in love with a fairy. Besides, a fairy always runs away from people. No, this love is not practical. It is not possible that a hawk becomes a chicken's friend, and no one has ever seen a fairy getting close to a human being. I could only bridle a fairy if I were Solomon.* So he left the pond and rode back to his men to rest.

It was strange that those two blossoms were torn from the spring; two thirsty souls hurt by water. She ran away from the water of the pond, and he fell in the well of sadness left by that water. Usually, people wash and refresh by the spring, and hard bread becomes soft in the water. This is true for all except the two who left the pond and looked toward tough days ahead.

CHAPTER 11

Shirin in Parviz's Castle

hirin left the pond without knowing that she was going away from Parviz instead of toward him. She went through hot, rough roads until she got to Tisfoon. She saw the tall fortifications which surrounded the capital. She entered the big gate to the city where the Persian Kings kept their winter palaces—some called Tisfoon the winter capital of the Persian Empire.

The city was magnificent. The small buildings were surrounded by gardens full of apple, date, fig and cyprus trees. She passed farms full of wheat and barley, melon vines, bean plants and large patches of lettuce. The roses were abundant on each side of the street with red poppies spread all over the orchards and gardens.

She could see the four-story building that was the Persian palace from a distance. It stood tall and magnificent. The splendor of the imperial palace complex at Tisfoon included Parviz's palace, Shâhigân-i Spêd, the white palace, and the grand arch, Taq-e-Kasra. The arch was flanked by façades decorated with blank arcading and pilasters. The castle was built with brick, and the pillars were decorated with marble; the jagged windows were decorated with copper, gold, and silver.

She was a Princess and used to luxuries, but the grandeur of the palace made her eyes widen. She removed her hood and rode straight toward the white castle. When she got there, she asked to see Parviz. The guards had been instructed by Parviz to welcome Shirin as his guest, so they let her inside. The palace was full of young Princes and Princesses. Usually, the youth liked to spend their time with those of their age and being in the palace where the Crown Prince was living had many advantages. The Princesses mostly were hoping to become his Majesty's favorite. When they saw Shirin enter, all the beautiful Princesses gathered around and started questioning her.

She asked, "Where is Parviz?"

They answered, "Oh, we think that he went hunting." Then they began asking her.

"Who are you?" one asked.

"Where have you come from?" another asked.

She did not dare to tell them the truth, so she said, "My story is very long. I can only say it to the Crown Prince. He will tell you himself why I am here. But this horse is a gem and needs to be kept in good condition since there is no horse like this one in this world."

When they heard what she said, they welcomed her as the royals do. They fastened the horse in the stables. Then the servant led her to a sumptuous bedroom with a private bath where she could wash up before he brought her down to dinner. She was happy when she heard their promise that her lover would be there soon, so she ate and slept deeply.

After several months of waiting, she finally heard that Parviz was off on a hunting trip, and no one knew where he was or when he'd be back. She realized that the rider who was looking at her in the pond for sure was Parviz. She became sad and blamed herself for running away from the hollow.

What should she do now? She could not go back to Armenia. She was not sure how her aunt would react since she had run away without her knowledge. She was not happy in the palace. Since with the arrival of summer, it was hot, and most of the Princes and Princesses were leaving Tisfoon to go to Ecbatana or Estakhr. Only a few servants remained, and they thought she was a bond-woman. She was okay with that and so she worked alongside them, but the weather was killing her. She was used to the cold weather of Armenia and Tisfoon in summer, to her, seemed like Hell. The weather was not her only problem though, the fact that she had left her dear aunt only to find her lover gone was so bothersome that she became ill.

CHAPTER 12

Parviz in Armenia

When Parviz left the spring and pond, he too became sad. His sadness increased as the distance from the lake increased. But he allowed himself the hope that finding Shirin will bring him the calmness he was seeking. *Since I am going to see Shirin I might find the sunshine*, he thought.

He passed the mountain like a fresh flower, and his aroma reached the authorities. The Kings of each province he crossed came to pay their respects and invite him to see their territory. He accepted their invitations, and from Kurdistan on he stayed a week or two in each territory. His charm and beauty, combined with his vast knowledge, amused them, and they treated him as their King.

He had so much fun seeing the people, feeling their excitement, being welcomed by his hosts that he forgot about his father's intention of killing him. He thought that it might be false news, and as all youth are, he became carefree and resumed being a Crown Prince as though nothing had happened. Surely if these Kings had not heard of his father's anger, then there was no use telling them. He was on a hunting trip and loved to see his country he told the authorities in those regions. It had been four months since he had run away from Tisfoon. When he got to Moghan, he stayed there for three weeks, then he went to Fakharzan.

Mahin-Bano heard that the Crown Prince was staying in a nearby city, so she decided to visit him. It was important for her to have the Crown Prince as a friend since East Armenia was one of the states in the Persian Empire at that time. She first sent a gift to him as it is customary. Parviz was exceedingly happy to hear the news that the Shah of Armenia was coming to see him. His goal was to go and find Shirin and possibly stay as the guest of the Shah of Armenia. His father would not try to kill him if he was so far away from the capital and in the country which was always getting threatened by their enemies. He did not mind it either, power and wealth are not usually as concerning to youths as the fun they could have in a beautiful place. So, he impatiently awaited her arrival. When she came, Parviz came down from his throne and welcomed her. They put a chair close to his throne for her to sit in.

"Your Majesty is well I hope," she asked?

Husrō-Parviz said, "Yes, thank you my dear Shah of Armenia. How are you doing? I hope you are enjoying each day. I brought you here as a guest, but I do not have all I can to entertain you since I am a guest here myself."

Mahin-Bano was very amused by his politeness and modesty. She said, "My King will be healthy. I am lucky to have you as our protector. I will be happy to be at your service no matter where you are."

She stayed with him for a week. One lovely day, they were sitting in an orchard full of intoxicating flowers and fruits. Parviz was as handsome as ever; his face had just started to grow a beard. The servants were bringing in fresh fruit, cookies, and wine. People were relaxing, and conversation flowed. Mahin-Bano bowed in front of the young Prince and said, "I have a request that you come to Barda and stay there all winter. Barda has a warmer climate, and you can rest and be my guest."

He answered, "That is an excellent idea. You go, and I will follow you." The next morning, they moved toward Barda. The place was beautiful, and they set up their tents everywhere in the beautiful pastures. Mahin-Bano entertained him, and the field gave him ample enjoyment by providing countless species of prey for their hunting activities. What was missing, and a mystery to him, was that there was no news about Shirin the beautiful idol he had come all this distance to eagerly meet. There were many beautiful girls around him, but he was attracted to none of them. He was in love with the painting in his mind and was not attracted to anyone else.

So, he busied himself with hunting during the days or had parties with music and wine at night. Only if he could find Shah-Pour, he would know if the girl he was in love was involved with someone else or not. Until then, he decided to wait.

CHAPTER 13

Shah-Pour Returns

One night, it was as beautiful as any Nowruz night which helped the sadness disappear better than had it been the actual New Year's night. Parviz was sitting on his throne and the room contained a big brazier with fire in the middle. His close friends were sitting around. Outside of the Shah's tent, the guards protected the camp from any danger. Inside the tent, the scent of ood (agarwood) and amber spread throughout. Armenian charcoal was burning inside the brazier. One mused, "People say that there is no color above black, but the black charcoal turns red in the fire."

An older gentleman said, "Well I guess the fire has learned this trick from Time, which turns my black hair to white." Everyone applauded this comment. The tent was decorated all over with different colored roses. Pomegranates and oranges were served on trays, and the beautiful ladies served red wine.

The musicians started playing the harp and singing the Pahlavi's cantos. The kamancheh was playing, and the singer was singing:

What a beautiful orchard would be the orchard of life!
If it was immune from the autumn winds.

44

The most magnificent palace would be the Palace of Life.
Only if it was everlasting and forever.
This beautiful place is not a good one
since as soon as you settle down it tells you to get up.
Since this Monastery of the Earth is not a stable place,
then drink wine and destroy it.
We have today to be sure of
even we are not certain to have today and tonight.
So, come and start it with laughter, drink wine
and keep making our lives, and the world, alive.
It is ok if we don't sleep one night
Since we will sleep aplenty after we die.

Husrō-Parviz was getting drunk, and the music filled the silence of the evening. A beautiful girl servant came in and said, "A man called Shah-Pour wants to come in. Should I let him or send him away?"

The Shah's heart boiled up with a steady beating. He wanted to jump up and run out of the tent to see his messenger of love, but he was a Prince and was trained to be calm at the most disturbing moments.

He said, "Oh yes, I was expecting him, let him in." Then he waved his hand to the musicians and said, "I want to retire now to attend an important meeting."

Everyone in the crowd stood up and bowed to say goodnight when Shah-Pour arrived. He bowed and stood until the tent was empty. The Prince descended his throne, took Shah-Pour's hand, and made him sit by him asking, "What happened? I was expecting you and Shirin several months ago! I am so anxious to know what happened to you and where has Shirin been? Since I've been here, I have not seen or heard of her."

"Long live my King, I hope your army is never defeated and has good luck today and every day. My story is long, and you might be tired this late at night, but I will tell you everything if you wish."

"Oh, I cannot wait to hear it, please go ahead and tell me everything. I don't care about sleeping tonight."

"Your wish is my command." Then Shah-Pour started telling him everything. He told about the meeting with Shirin and tricking her to go to his palace. There was a roar from Parviz's heart, and he said, "Please tell me about her, how did she look?"

"My King, I was smart, but I think your luck helped me too. I spied on her with a hunter's eyes. I saw a goddess who was ingenious and beautiful. Her hair was so pretty that you would think that Christ had settled there to cure sicknesses.

"Her face was as lovely as the almond blossoms and her skin as white as the skinless almond. Her body was like two worlds fastened by a thin hair in the middle. Her mouth was so attractive; I do not think anyone had kissed her lips save for the mirror when she was in her cups. Her hands have touched nothing but her own hair. Although she is making all the men madly in love with her, she is madly in love with my King. I encouraged her to leave here with Shabdiz, but I got sick and could not catch her myself. I know now that she has reached the Shahzadeh's palace."

Husrō-Parviz got up and hugged him and gave him a present. Then he was struck with the realization that the woman he saw at the pond was not a fairy but his love.

He said, "I was told to leave the capital for a few months until my father's anger cooled down and I did not want to spend this time anywhere but Armenia. Unfortunately, she did not recognize me and went away as fast as the wind; we left in two different directions. Now I want you to return to Tisfoon and bring her back to me."

"Your wish is my command, if I have a good horse, I can bring her here in less than a month."

CHAPTER 14

Shah-Pour on His Way to Tisfoon

The best days of our life are the days of our youth. Parviz, who was chieftain of the world, was youthful and a happy young man. He would not drink without music. He would not have fun without players and singers.

The day after seeing Shah-Pour, he was sitting in his tent with a glass of wine when Mahin-Bano came to visit. Parviz welcomed her and sat closer to her than ever before. At lunchtime, he said his prayers, and then he drank wine with her. When he became drunk, he brought the conversation to Shirin.

"I heard that you had a niece who looked like a laughing flower and was very brave! I heard that her horse spirited her off and made her disappear."

Mahin-Bano sighed and said with a tear in her eyes. "That is true, and I am sick from her disappearance and know not what to do. I am frightened to find out what happened to her. That is why I did not ask my men to search for her. I carry little hope that maybe someday she will come back to me."

Husrō-Parviz smiled and said, "I understand your concerns and see the sadness it has been causing you. But I have good news;

she seems to be alive. Today someone told me that he knows where she is. I am sending him to see if he can bring her back."

Mahin-Bano fainted. When she came to, she sat on the ground and started to kiss his feet while tears ran down her face. "Oh, if I could see her just one minute and then die; I would accept my death sentence just to be able to see her face."

Husrō-Parviz, who felt responsible for her pain, took hold of her elbow and helped her get up. He said, "I am so sorry to disturb you. But now you should be happy that she is alive. I will send my man to fetch her and bring her here in less than two months. So be happy and enjoy life."

She kissed his hand and said, "I hope that the moon will kiss your hand. The west and the east will be at your service. I know that when you came to this land that my luck came with you. Since you are with me, I know that anything is possible. If you are sending anyone to fetch her, let me know. I like to give him Golgoon. It is Shabdiz' double. No horse can catch up with Shabdiz except Golgoon."

"It is generous of you to give such an expensive gift."

"Oh, nothing is more important to me than seeing my beloved niece as soon as possible."

"All right then, he is ready to leave immediately. We will send someone with you to get the horse."

"Thank you, Your Majesty; I will be in debt to you all my life."

"Please do not mention it, you have been a good host to me, and I love to see you happy."

Someone went with Mahin-Bano and brought Golgoon to Shah-Pour. Shah-Pour took both his horse and Golgoon and started the long trip to Tisfoon.

When he got to Tisfoon, he went to Parviz's castle, showed his pass, and went to the palace where Shirin was living. When he went in, he could hardly recognize her. He bowed and told her, "I hope My Lady will be healthy and victorious in everything she does. I would like to know how Your Majesty is and how you overcame the bad and rough road to the capital?"

Shirin, who had recovered from her sickness and was getting used to the Tisfoon's weather with the arrival of fall, said, "As you instructed me I left my place and all my friends to come here and find my Prince Charming. Instead, I found jealous Princesses and was treated like a servant. Then they all left, and I was left with the intolerable heat to get sick. What happened to that Prince of yours who was madly in love with me? Now I cannot go back to my homeland, and I am miserable here."

"I understand your anger Your Majesty, I did not lie to you. My Lord is madly in love with you, but he was in danger and had to run for his life. Have you heard about the King's anger? If not, you should know that Parviz left the Iranian Plateau and is in Armenia now."

Shirin was stunned. She came to Tisfoon, and he went to Armenia! Wow! She frowned and said, "No I did not hear anything a stranger should not hear. Who threatened his life and when?"

Shah-Pour looked at her pale face and said, "According to the stories I heard, it was some misunderstanding where the King thought Parviz was rebelling against him. So, the King decided to imprison him, but Parviz's friend let him know of the danger, so he left Tisfoon. He wanted to be with you, so he rode fast toward Armenian soil about six months ago."

A sigh escaped her mouth. The scenery of the pond with a tall, beautiful man mounting a horse appeared in front of her eyes. She thought then that he looked like the picture she saw in the painting but did not pay attention to her inner thoughts. If she had not run away from that pond in such a hurry, she would not have gone through so much hardship. She did not say a word. She was in so much agony about her actions that she couldn't bring herself to speak.

Shah-Pour broke the silence. "I know you went through a hard time but from this harshness of life, you will be happy. I was ill and could not reach you. When I became better, I heard that Parviz was in Armenia. I went there and saw him. He asked me to come for you and take you there. Your aunt gave us Golgoon so you can ride him on the way back."

Shirin's screams of joy filled the room. "My aunt is forgiving me and sent her favorite horse for me?"

"My Lady, of course, she has. She had given up hope of your wellness and is now so happy that she will see you alive again."

Shirin was delighted that both of her beloved were waiting for her and wanted her home. The next morning Shirin mounted upon Golgoon's back and left Tisfoon for Armenia with Shah-Pour.

CHAPTER 15

Rebel in the Court

etween June 589 to February of 590, or the time Parviz left Tisfoon to the day Shirin left Tisfoon, there was a revolt shaping up against Shah-Hanshah Hormozd. There were several reasons; he was very rigid about the law and justice, the long war against their neighbors made the citizens vulnerable, and the people were growing poor while the nobles grew very wealthy. The Shah decided to side with those without power or voices and he demanded that the rich pay more taxes. He gave that tax money to the poor.

There was another problem in his twenty years of reign. Zoroastrianism was the official religion of the state under Sassanid's era, and the religious establishment had gained considerable power. Since most Persians were Zoroastrian, this was not a problem. But with the conversion of the Roman Empire to Christianity and the spread of its religion throughout the Persian Empire, the religious leaders complained that the Persian Christians were Roman spies who should be restricted.

The Shah did not accept the argument and told them, "A chair will not be able to stand on only two legs, but it needs four legs to be stable. A country neither can survive if we base it on only one religious group. So, I will let other religions spread through my Empire and will punish anyone who tries to hurt the Christians."

The Mobeds (ranking Zoroastrian clerics) did not like this policy and started a campaign against the Shah. He, in turn, fought back by imprisoning or killing them.

The more he stressed justice for all, the more high-ranking officials from the religious establishment and armies became dissatisfied. Opposition to his decisions grew louder. He was managing until they made him suspicious of his Crown Prince; then his luck changed. Their trick worked, and he had decided to put Parviz in jail. The morning after Parviz left Tisfoon he was angered by his son's absence and resolved that someone should have told him. So, he ordered the arrest of his brothers-in-law, all of Parviz's friends, and the families from his mother's side. The order did not fall silently since most of the high-ranking authorities went to jail. The rumor about his Crown Prince being disappointed and leaving his father's palace spread across the country. While in his summer palace, the Shah's enemies started to regroup. By the time, he came back to Tisfoon most nobles had agreed that he was no longer fit to rule. Some said that Bahram was coming to take over the capital; the opposition said Parviz was gathering troops and would return. Others still said that the Shah should not rule since he was trying to kill his son. The news penetrated the jail; Parviz's uncles, Gostham, and Bandoy heard these rumors, so they bribed the guards and broke out of jail. As military officers, they were able to get the troops to agree that they should overthrow the Shah and choose a new leader. With military agreement, they attacked the palace, captured, and blinded Shah Hormozd.

CHAPTER 16

Parviz Hears the Devastating News

*H*usrō-Parviz was sitting in his tent one day drinking and thinking of Shirin and the moment of their meeting when a messenger came to his door. He bowed and said, "Long live my King. The Shah-Hanshah of Persia had been blinded."

Parviz jumped up and said, "What are you talking about?"

"My King, they blinded him. Life has given him a cane instead of a sword, and he no longer can see, so we have to obey your commands now." He bowed again.

Parviz could not believe this! He fell back on his throne remembering his father's kind eyes and was unable to say a word. Yes, he ran away for a rumor that one of his father's close friends brought to him, but he never thought that there was any real threat. He was too close to his father to rejoice in his blindness. There was a profound silence in the court for a few minutes. The messenger broke it, saying, "I have some letters for you, if you permit me I will deliver them."

"Yes, give them but first, tell me who did it?"

He bowed and said, "My King, from what I heard your uncles,

Gostham and Bandooy, have blinded him and proclaimed you the King."

Husrō-Parviz took the letters and told the man to go rest. The messenger left, and he began to read the letters. They were from his uncles and his other close relatives and friends. They all stressed that he should come to capital as soon as he could. "If you have dirty hair do not wash it, if you are talking, stop and leave immediately. It is important that you come at once since if you don't come quickly, it might be too late." He realized that he had a heavy duty to follow, whether he liked it or not.

One of his friends by the name of Mehrdad came in and saw him drowning in his thoughts. He said, "I see my King deep in his thoughts, what is bothering you? What can I do to cheer you up?"

Husrō-Parviz looked at his friend standing in front of him waiting for his reply. "Sit down my friend and know that no one can make me happy today since I heard horrible news and did not know how to swallow it." Then he told him about the messenger and the letters.

Mehrdad, who was as shocked as Parviz, said, "I understand your agony and sorrow for the great King. But this is how life is, and the weather on this dirty planet has its ups and downs. Sometimes life is like a bee, and sometimes it is like honey. It has kindness and anger; you wash away the bitterness with sweets. Now you have a duty to tend this enormous country of yours, and you need to be patient and be smart."

Parviz heard his friend and agreed that he had to rush to Tisfoon to see what he could do with the problem in the capital.

CHAPTER 17

Parviz Becomes Shah-Hanshah

Ousrō-Parviz arrived in Tisfoon, and everyone from nobility to peasants welcomed him. He sat on the throne and announced, "This throne is given to me by God, and I should obey His command. I shall do nothing but good for my people since an unjust King will only bring his people troubles. I am a friend to everyone and do not want to get involved in a war with any of you. I have accepted this throne from God, and I ask you to obey the law. Do not hurt people or take their belongings. I will follow the proper path and avoid the wrong as long as I live. I will not judge anyone who has been after my throne. Do not worry, you deserve security in your life, and I am here to guarantee that security."

Those who heard his speech said it was well done, and they were happy. When darkness arrived, the Shah came down from his throne and went to see his father. His heart was full of pain. He bent down and kissed his father's hand. He said, "My King, you know that if I were here, I would not have let anyone hurt you. Now tell me what I should do. I am here in your service and will do whatever you wish. If you order me, I will be a servant in your court. I will not accept the Kingdom and will cut my head off for you."

Hormozd felt his son's tears on his hand. He listened to what his son said and realized that he was sincere. What happened had not been Parviz's plan, so Hormozd opened his arms and embraced his son, ashamed for his own insecurity in wanting to imprison a son so kind. "My son I will be okay with this pain. I am glad that they chose you as their King. It was my plan anyway to give my throne to you on my death bed. Now I am alive and will hear what kind of King you will be.

"I have three demands and not more. First, I want you to stop by and talk to me every night, so my ears feel joy at hearing your voice. Also, send me an old champion from the war who was a good hunter to come and talk to me about his adventures.

"Second, send me someone who can read and knows about the old Kingdoms and Kings to read for me and make me busy picturing them in my mind.

"Third, I want you to make your uncles blind and revenge my pain with the same action."

Parviz said, "Oh my King, I will obey your wishes and will be here every night to talk to you. I also will send someone each day to talk about their adventures and those of the previous Kings for you to enjoy. I do not want to see anyone remain alive who hurt you, but we have to be careful. Today we have an enemy like Bahram Choobin with thousands of men in his army. If I kill Gostham, I will not live long. You should know by now that putting them in jail caused this revolt. We will not be better off if I harm them today. You know that the will of God did this. Otherwise, nobody could hurt you. I will remember your request and seek your revenge when I am strong enough."

He stayed with his father a long time, until it was late at night, then said goodbye and left with a tear in his eye. When he arrived home, he went directly to his bedchamber, changed and went to sleep.

All of a sudden, he remembered that Shirin was staying in the palace. Did she leave with Shah-Pour or is she still here? He wondered. The next morning, he asked the maid about her.

"Yes, she was here but left with Shah-Pour. But she left her horse Shabdiz for you. We thought that you requested her to leave!"

Parviz's heart was full of sorrow. Being away from the love of his life was not easy. He had not planned to be in Tisfoon, but destiny brought him back with big responsibilities on his shoulders. He left Armenia a few days after Shirin left Tisfoon. What could be done? His duty was to his country and his people, but his heart was with Shirin and wanted so much to fly back and have her with him. Well, he told himself when things calmed down he would marry her and make her his Queen. He had Shabdiz to remind him of Shirin. To remember the moon of his life, he would visit the black horse every night.

He took care of daily administrative work. But as any young man would, he put aside some time to spend with his friends drinking or hunting. He was a good ruler, and people were generally pleased with him.

CHAPTER 18

Shirin Returns to Mahin-Bano

When Shirin got to Armenia, they found out that Parviz had to leave in a hurry. Shah-Pour took her to Mahin-Bano's castle. Nobody could measure Mahin-Bano's joy. She was like an old woman who has reclaimed her youth, or someone who dies and returns to life. She hugged Shirin and kissed her many times. Her nannies and nurses and her friends and family gathered around her, hugged and kissed her then thanked God for her return. They all gave gifts to the fire temple for her safety.

Mahin-Bano did everything to make her happy. She gave her jewelry and properties and told her, "You can do whatever you want to do with them." She did not ask her any questions since she knew the reason for her disappearance—she had wanted to pursue her love. She knew it because after talking with the Shah she felt there was something between he and her niece. She had asked Shirin's friends, and they told her about the painting and her long talks with Shah-Pour. Mahin-Bano just gave her more love so she could soothe the pain of separation. So, Shirin gathered each of her forty friends, and they restarted the frolicking and fun they used to have.

CHAPTER 19

Nizami Recounts Parviz's Wars

*H*ere the poet, Nizami, stopped and grabbed a thick book saying: "I am going to read from *Shahnameh* which was written hundreds of years before me. Ferdowsi, the great epic writer, wrote many love stories, but when he started to talk about Shah Parviz, he was too tired and old to write about Parviz's love and instead only detailed his wars. I will read about Parviz's wars from this book since I do not want to repeat what he wrote." So, Nizami rubbed on his long bear and started to read.

When Bahram heard the news that Parviz was crowned after Hormozd had been blinded, he felt surprised and downtrodden. He thought his trick would make the Shah kill his son and the people would turn against him leaving room for Bahram to take advantage of the muddy water and get his wish.

Now the young and beloved Crown Prince was the King. Bahram thought for a while and decided that he needed to act fast if he wanted the Persian Kingdom. He decided to start a rumor that Parviz was the one who blinded his father. He wrote a letter to others in the court. "You cannot trust this child to govern the Persian Empire. You cannot deign the country to be ruled by a person who blinded his own father. To him, a mere sip of wine is the same color as the holy fire, and it is much better than the blood of hundreds of brothers. He will give away our country to the sound of music; he loves singing better than this entire country. He is just a boy who does not know good from bad. You should kill him right now and find another King who can rule or, if it is better, put him in jail. You start the motion, and I will come to finish him." Then he gathered more people under his command and went to Nahravan.

When Parviz heard of Bahram's actions, he was grieved by his bad luck. He sent informants to discover how many were under Bahram's command and how loyal they were. He wanted to know about Bahram's habits, and how he treated his men. He learned there were many in Bahram's army, and they were all loyal. No one, not even the high-ranking generals, seemed to question his decisions. He had his advisers and ruled like a king. At night, he consulted the Kelileh-va-Damaneh, the book all Kings consulted.

Parviz gathered his advisors and army officers, people like Gostham, Bandooy, Radian, and others, and said, "We have a big job in front of us. Bahram is a superior army officer and is brave in wars against his enemies. He has learned all of the Kingdom's customs and behaviors from my father. He has good advisors too. Now you tell me what we should do since I am younger than all of you. I want to hear your suggestions."

The Mobed told him, "I hope you will be happy all your days. You should know that when God created us, he divided wisdom into four parts. God gave half of it to the King, gave the third part to the pious, and the fourth part, to the army with the King. Wisdom does not belong to non-believers; I hope you can understand what I say."

Parviz said, "Oh, how I would like to write your advice in gold since the words of Mobeds are like gems. However, I have something else to say. When the two armies face each other, I will not be ashamed to go in front of his army and call Bahram out. I will ask him for peace and show him kindness and praise him. If he accepts, it will be a triumph since he is a brave general and we need him. If he does not agree with the truth, then I will fight him with all of our might."

Everyone agreed that his solution would be the best. They praised him and called him the King of the Earth. They told him, "We wish you greatness and victory. We hope you never see defeat in your life." With this, Parviz led his troops out of Tisfoon. When they drew close to Nahravan, the two armies faced each other. Bahram was riding a piebald horse with three Turkish men at his side covered in his armor.

Husrō-Parviz, Gostham, Barzin, and Bandooy were each covered with armor too.

When Bahram saw the Shah, he complained to his compatriots that, "This bastard who is lazy and slow got all the King's wealth? Now I will kill him. If you look at his army, you can't find a man who can fight me and win." He then started riding toward the Shah with a few Persians who were under his command.

Parviz asked his supporters, "Which one is Bahram?"

Gordooy (another oficer) told him "My King, do you see that man who is riding that glorious horse, who wears white clothing with a black baldric?

Shah-Hanshah said, "That tall, smoky-colored man who is sitting on that piebald horse?"

"Yes, that is him, you see him with a pig nose and sleepy eyes? It seems that he has anger toward the world. He never did any good in his life; he is the enemy of God and humanity."

Parviz said, "I see he has many men under him, and no one

knows who will be defeated. I will do all in my power to prevent a civil war if possible. I will talk to him, and if he agrees, I will assign him as governor of one of the Persian States. It is better to start the negotiation than getting lazy in the war. It is important for me to prevent the killing of any of our men if we can."

Gostham said, "I wish you happiness all your life. You do what you think you should do. You are just, and he is an injustice; you are all brain, and his head is full of wind."

Parviz went in front of the army and called Bahram. "Oh, general why are you at war with your King? You are the champion of your country. You are the pillar of our army when in war and a bright candle when in shindig. I have asked about you and know all of your good qualities. I would like to invite you and your army to be my guests, and I will make you the commander-in-chief of the Persian army."

Bahram said, "I am happy, and my life cannot be better. I don't see the nobleness in you. You don't know what a Kingdom, justice, or injustice is. I will soon make a tall gallows and will fasten your hands and hang you so you can see the bitterness of your life."

When Parviz heard his answer, he turned as white as a jasmine blossom, but said, "Ungrateful man, only unfaithful people talk like this. You curse the guests coming to you from a distance instead of welcoming them! This is not how Kings or officers behave. I haven't heard either Persians or Arabs act like this for last three hundred years. Don't you know that I am your King, and you should obey my orders? Am I not the son of Hormozd and grandson of Anoshiravan? Who is more suitable to be a King than me?"

Bahram said, "You are a bad sign, and your behavior is stupid. You talk about being a guest, you are an evil nature, and your story is old-fashioned. What are you saying by being a King? You are not clever and not a champion of war. There is no one more sinful than you. Your father was a just King and never hurt another.

You did not respect the great man and blinded him so you could take his throne. I will take his revenge. I will kill you and become King myself. I will be a just and brave King. You blinded a King and have those who did it helping you. You are not a King or even a noble person. I said you should not live in this world. Since the Iranians are your enemy, they will destroy you. They will cut off your flesh and give your bones to their dogs. They will call me King. No, I will not silently live while you are walking on the ground."

Husrō-Parviz said, "I do not know why you are getting angry and demanding more than you deserve. It is not okay for a man to use foul words; it seems that wisdom has fled your brain and that is why you speak the way you do. Usually, when bad fortune strikes a person, he begins talking nonsense. I do not want a champion like you. It is wise if you kick your anger. You are adamant and a real army officer. You could be my right hand. But it seems that you want the Kingdom instead, and we will know soon what God's wish is. I am not sure who taught you such a satanic idea, but whoever it was they desire your destruction and death."

He then turned away and went to his tent and took off his crown and started praying. He said, "My God, you know everything; please let me see what I should do. If this Kingdom is going to be destroyed, then let me know, so I do not fight and instead stay in the fire temple and serve you. If this Kingdom is mine, then please help me and my army to defeat the enemy and I will give as much as I can to fire temple. I will give 10,000 drams if I become the King." He prayed then changed his clothing and went to the war zone. He and Bahram exchanged some more words, and the war started.

One of the Turks threw his lasso at the King; its noose caught the top of his head, and Gostham cut the rope without any injury befalling the King. But there were many killed that day and the killing continued on and on until the dawn when they all returned to their tents.

When Bahram entered his tent, he was tired and upset. His sister went to him and said, "What happened in the fight? I know that King Parviz is young and might be quick to judge, but you should be wise and ask for the truth."

Bahram said, "You should not call him the King. He is not wise nor a war hero. The King needs to have accomplishments, not just be born a Prince."

The wise sister told him, "I have told you so many times, but you are not listening to me. You probably have heard that the right advice is bitter; the person who tells you your faults tells you the truth. Do not destroy your city and yourself. None of your ancestors have been a King. If this young man dies, his father is still alive. You are playing with fire and will lose your head. I do not know what will happen, but both of my eyes are full of tears. You will not get anything but pain. Your name will be called an evil omen, and you will burn in Hell. Can't you see that you are here because King Hormozd gave you an army to fight the Chinese? That made you victorious, but now you lust to be a King. Don't you remember the history of warriors like Rostam and Saam who were victorious in so many wars? They did not try to become King. Do you want to become King after one victory? When Shah Hormozd got mad, you were supposed to be patient. Now that he is blind, and his son came from Barda, you should go to the new King. You had everything, why do you have to go after the crown?"

Bahram said, "Your advice is wise, but I cannot change the course of events now."

When Parviz went back that night, he called all his knights and told them, "You have been loyal to my ancestors, and I have not seen anything but good from you. I want to tell you a secret;

I have seen Bahram, who is a brave knight. He calls me a child and scares me with his sword. He does not know that I will attack him tonight. You should not tell this to anyone otherwise we will be defeated." They all said they would be with him whatever he ordered them to do. When he retired to his tent with his close acquaintances, Gostham and Bandooy started talking about his plan for attacking that night.

Gostham said, "Why are you ignorant of the circumstances? Attacking them at night turns your own army against you. This is a civil war. There are sons whose fathers are in the enemy's camp. And fathers whose sons are there. How are you expecting them to fight for you? You made a mistake telling all the knights about your plan. Now we will get defeated for sure."

Bandooy said, "We cannot do anything about past events. This is war, and there will be fighting. But I agree with Gostham that they might know of our plan, and I don't want you to be here with the army tonight. The Shah liked his suggestion so he took a few of his bravest generals and went to a place on a hill where he could see the army from a distance."

Bahram sent a man who was a good talker, with a good sense of reasoning, to go to his relatives in Parviz's camp and tell them to leave Parviz and join Bahram. The families answered, "We will not leave Parviz since we think that he will eventually succeed, but be careful since he is going to attack tonight. So, do not stay in that camp." The man went back and told Bahram what he heard. They started fires all over the camp and got ready for the attack.

When Parviz's army attacked, the enemy was ready. A huge battle ensued. There were many killed and everyone began asking, "Where is King Parviz now?"

It was almost dawn when Parviz, watching from a distance, told his companions that he should be there. He went down to the battle and drew his sword. He killed one of Bahram's knights and told his army to fight a little longer. But his soldiers were tired, and they had all heard the rumor that Parviz was the one who blinded his father. So, they did not listen, but instead left the battleground.

Parviz told Bandooy, "Now I am getting afraid. I have no children, and if I die, there will be no King for the Persian land."

Bandooy said, "I hope that never happens, but because your army has left, you should not stay since no one is your friend now."

He told Zangoy, "Go and find those who are still in the camp and gather about one thousand and pack everything in the camp including my tent and my crown and take them to the bridge."

Bahram arrived, and Parviz and Bahram began to fight. Their battle lingered, and neither one was able to defeat the other. When the sun started to disappear, Zangoy came and told Parviz, "We packed everything, and everyone is on the bridge now." When he heard this news, he told Gostham that since Bahram's army was large, it was not wise to stay and die.

He headed towards the bridge, but Bahram followed him. When he mounted the bridge, Parviz asked for his bow and started to shoot at the army following him. He killed many soldiers, but Bahram was after him like an angry tiger.

Parviz shot and hit Bahram's horse, which dropped and died. Bahram grabbed his shield as one of his officers hoisted him upon his horse and fled the bridge with his army following. Then Parviz moved toward Tisfoon, taking out the bridge so Bahram's army could not reach them. He also closed all the gates to the city and made a big speech, trying to reassure his people. Then, he went to see his father. He told him all about the fight and the fact that his army left him. "My King, the man that you made a knight is living like a King. He has raised a big army. I tried to reason with him, but that proved fruitless. He was mad and wanted war. There was a battle, and many lost their lives. My army left me, and they are calling him a King. I decided to leave rather than stay and get killed. He is close behind, near the bridge. I have considered the matter, and I think the best way is for me to leave and go to the Arab's to retrieve some help. What do you say?"

His father answered that, "This is not the right thing to do. They are not going to help you since you do not have any power. There is no benefit for them to help you. They might even give you to your enemy. Your support now is from God. If you want to leave the country, then go fast toward Roman territory. The Emperor is your relative, and he has money and an army to help you. Tell him I was the one who suggested this to you."

Husrō-Parviz kissed his father's hand and said, "Long live my King. I will do what you suggested."

He told Gostham and Bandooy that they would be leaving the capital and going to the Romans. They packed and left the city. They were far from the city when he saw that his uncles were not coming as fast. He rode towards them and asked, "What is going on? Why are you moving so slowly? You know that Bahram is going to follow us."

Gostham said, "Do not worry about Bahram since his black flag is far away. In truth, we do not agree with this decision. When Bahram comes to the capital, he will give your father the Kingdom and Hormozd will write the Roman Empire to arrest you and send you to him."

Parviz said, "He will not do that to me. But even if is so, I must go since I have no other choice. If it is the will of God to imprison me or kill me, I will agree with His will." He then kicked his horse and galloped toward the west.

CHAPTER 20

Parviz Reaches the Land of His Lover

Nizami closed Ferdowsi's book of wars from which he'd been reading and began his own story once again:

Parviz went to Azerbaijan and from there to Moghan. The closer he got to the land of his lover the more excited he became. Hunting was one of his favorite sports, and in its way, it helped him survive the journey. If he could hunt enough for their consumption, he had less need to pay for his army's food. He did not know how long he would be away from his throne, but he had to provide for the men who risked their lives to support him on this long and hard trip. How long the money he had with him would last, he did not know.

On a day designated for hunting, he saw a cloud of dust in the distance indicating there was someone else in the hunting grounds. He was alone in his corner when he saw the fairy from the water so many months earlier.

Shirin and her friends had also decided to go hunting that day. The bright sunlight of an early spring streamed shafts down the tall trees, and the perfume of narcissus mingled with the earthy scent of freshly disturbed soil when Shirin spotted an athletic man astride an enormous black horse. Each in their way glorious examples of blue-blooded pedigree, perfect specimens of muscle tone, she had no doubt this time that the handsome man she spotted could only be the King of the Persian Empire. He was her only love. Tall, dark, and quite indecently good-looking he was riding her beloved Shabdiz.

The two hunters flew to each other as thirsty people who had just spotted water. Shabdiz and Golgoon flew toward each other like they understood the fire of their riders' passion. By this time, from two directions, their armies approached but waited for each leader.

Man and woman were both were hypnotized by the shock of seeing the other unexpectedly. For a while, none could move until Shirin finally spoke. She dismounted her horse bowed and said, "Oh My Lord, welcome to our territory. I hope the King of Kings is healthy and happy."

Parviz, who had dismounted at the same time said, "Hello to the most beautiful lady on Earth, Princess Shirin. Am I right?"

"Yes, My Lord, I am one of your vassals. You, who has thousands of serfs like me, are master to the seven regions of Persia. Because of your generosity, we have a castle. If My Lord accepts my invitation, it will be my greatest honor to attend you there."

Parviz said, "If you accept guests, I will be more than happy to accept your invitation."

Shirin bowed again and said, "You honor my aunt and I with your acceptance, My Lord. It is our greatest pleasure to have you at our palace."

Then she sent two riders to tell Mahin-Bano about the Shah's arrival.

When Mahin-Bano heard that the Shah was coming, she arranged a welcome committee which went out of their way to organize a grand reception for the King. It was late by the time they reached Mahin-Bano and her committee.

Parviz was happy to see Mahin-Bano again. She offered one of her castles for him and his men to stay. She also sent a group of cooks and servants to serve them as was right for their King. The dinner was ready in the castle, and after eating, Parviz and his men were tired from the long trip, so they welcomed Mahin-Bano's suggestion to wash and relax there for the night.

CHAPTER 21

Mahin-Bano's Advice to Shirin

At the dinner, Mahin-Bano realized from the way Parviz and Shirin looked at each other that they were in love, so she decided to speak to Shirin about it. She told Shirin that night, "My dear daughter, you are prettier than any-one in the world and the smartest and the bravest of all women. You are a jewel and very naïve. Life is full of tricks, the pearls get stolen, and the life gets ruined. I think that this young King is in love with you which is a great thing, and we should be proud of it. However, don't be fooled by his sweet talk, and do not get involved with him so much that it brings you shame. I heard that there are thousands of ladies in love with him, and they all are beautiful and smart. However, if he likes a jewel that he cannot have for free, he will not refuse to buy it. When he sees your good behavior, he will ask me for your hand as is our custom. Then you will be the Queen of this great land. If he is a King of Kings, we will be one of his Kings. If you become drunk and let him have you, then you will be disgraced by the world. There have been so many flowers who've been cut while fresh, but when they lose their aroma, they're thrown away. There have been wines in glasses, but after they are tasted, the rest is tossed out. You should know that getting married is much better than lovemaking."

Shirin said, "I swear to the seven bright stars in the sky and to the book of God that if I die of his love, I will not get too close to him unless he is my husband."

Mahin-Bano, who was happy with what she heard, told her, "Well then you can talk to him and hunt with him as long as you are not alone. Try to be with other people at all times while you visit. Also, you should encourage him to get his throne back because if he stays here and marries you he will resent it later and you will no longer be his favorite."

The next day when the sun started to shine the forty girls came to Shirin. Each was a warrior who could shoot an arrow as well as any ancient hero. They could play Chogan (polo) so nimbly that they could steal the ball from any opponent.

Ready, they fastened their bows and arrows to their waistlines and sat on their horses. Then, they went to see the Shah.

When they got to the castle, the chamberlain came out and led them in. They each bowed to the King and gave their greetings.

Parviz got up and answered their greeting then held Shirin's hand and took her to his throne. He asked her to sit at the chair on his right. Analyzing her entourage, he saw they were witty charmers as sweet as sugar and as beautiful as young girls should be. What he did not know was that they also possessed power and bravery and knew how to ride and hunt. However, by far the most beautiful ornament at the gathering was Shirin. The young King had forgotten all his troubles and all he wanted was to be with her. They conversed for a while; then he asked her if she would like to ride in the pastures in front of the castle?

Shirin said, "Sure I'd love to ride this beautiful spring morning."

They mounted their horses and went to the square. When they got to the green pastures, the fairy women went flying with joy.

When Parviz saw that the girls rode better than his men he asked Shirin, "What do you think if we play Chogan in this pasture?"

Shirin, smiling, said, "That is a marvelous idea; I love to play. One side will be my girls and I, and the other will be you and your men."

So, they started the game as was custom. Those on her side were the moon and her stars. The opposition were the Shah and his armies as the sun and its rays. There was tremendous excitement in the pasture. They played lion and deer. Then pheasants and hawks. One side was the hunter, and the other tried to escape. They alternated roles back and forth.

Sometimes the sun won the game, and the other times the moon. Sometimes Shirin gave up her pawns and sometimes the Shah. They played all day and went to the castle at night.

The next day they went hunting. Parviz was amused by the girls' fast riding. The day passed with excitement and joy and the night was spent drinking and listening to music while watching the Armenian dancers.

Parviz's attention though was always on Shirin. He saw deer eyes and a graceful body. Indeed, this was a deer who was hunting him! She was a drunken gazelle who had captured a lion. Shah Parviz, who was the best hunter in the world, became her prey.

The next morning, they returned to their frolicking, and this time, the game was to go into the wilderness and hunt. The hunting trip was as amusing as the Chogan game since Shirin and her girls shot as many deer and zebra as the men. Each one of the ladies proved a warrior on the hunting spree.

Each day was the same, playing Chogan and going hunting. A month passed from the day Parviz joined his love and he wanted to be alone with Shirin to tell her his feelings. With so many people around there was no way they could do anything but engage in pleasantries. When she left at night, he felt lonely and sad.

Parviz told Shirin one night, "Oh Queen of beauty, let's bring wine and have fun. Have music playing to get rid of any sadness. If we are happy or sad, we are not immune to the destruction of the life. Since we all will die someday, it is better to have fun than be sad."

Shirin gave him a beautiful smile, and put her fingers on her eyes and said, "It certainly is." Then she bowed and said good night.

Parviz could not wait for the night to become day so he could see the moon of his life again.

CHAPTER 22

The King's Merriment

Spring is the season of rainbow colors. Old and young trees are covered with green leaves and beautiful blossoms. So many lovers remember their long-lost loves this season. Buds are blooming everywhere. The army of birds is singing for their beloved flowers. The pansies are languid, and the red rose is drunk. Jasmine is the bearer of wine, and narcissus is the cup in hand.

The breeze roars over the carpet of field poppies. The weather throws the jewelry of petals on the green grass. Young deer play with their mothers and grow drunk with gentle maternal caresses.

The colorful birds spread their wings. On each branch, one spies the buds of new life, each flower bestowing its beauty. The sounds of nightingales plunder lovers' patience. In a season like this, it is wrong if you are not in love.

Parviz and Shirin day and night were merry and carefree anywhere they went. Sometimes they drank wine in the meadow, other times they picked flowers on the mountain. They passed plants and trees with a cup of wine and reached the Shahrood intoxicated. They led horses by the edge of the river and sat down to listen to it sing its songs.

Husrō-Parviz told Shirin that "The sweetness of your smile has transformed the cane of Shahrood's river into sugar cane. Your beauty steals this place just like the spring rain takes the pearl from the oyster. Sugar is bitter compared to your honey seasoned lips."

Shirin laughed and said, "Your stature in the royal court is like the cypress which gives the flowering trees a stern look."

Parviz chuckled and said, "I think if any of these beautiful flowers could look at your eyes they would uproot themselves out of jealousy. I am a slave bent to your ear."

Shirin laughed and said, "I have not heard of any King being a poet. As brave you are, you speak like song."

CHAPTER 23

Killing the Lion in the Meadow

One day the King suggested they go and see the scenery, although truthfully, he just wanted to watch the beautiful Shirin. They found a place to rest on the grass, in front of a pasture covered with irises. They stopped in that heavenly place and set up the royal court for the King. The servants around the court revolved like stars around the moon. Parviz and Shirin were sitting and enjoying their gathering. The red wine was given to them by the cupbearer. Parviz laughed and said, "I hope this joy will last forever."

The wine and the love collaborated, and the King became drunk on the two liquors. All of a sudden, a lion ran out of the woods, raising a smoke of dust into the air. Like a mad drunk, he attacked the army, and the military men started to run away. The lion moved like a whirlwind toward Parviz.

Husrō-Parviz had no knife or sword. However, he walked toward the lion. He cocked his fist to his ear and then forcefully struck the lion's temple. The punch was so powerful that he knocked the lion unconscious. Then he ordered his men to cut off its head and skin it.

From that day on it became customary that the Kings had to

wear a weapon with them to parties all the time. Although Parviz had a lion-like body and was a powerful King, his ability to fight a lion with his bare hand arose because he was drunk. His courage came from his drunkenness.

When the lion had attacked, the Princess Shirin felt frightened for her beloved's life. She trembled like a leaf in the wind. After he hit the lion, and his army cut off its head, Shirin went to Parviz and kissed his hand for doing such a brave job. She wet her mouth with rose water and her kiss covered the King's hand with sugar.

Parviz said, "Your kiss was sugar, but sugar should be in the mouth not on the hand." He then kissed her lips and said, "This is honey, and this is where you kiss." This was the first sweet cup delivering the message from Parviz to Shirin. Although she received a hundred more cups, she never forgot that first one. The first cup of wine you drink is much more fragrant tasting than the following cups. The first flower blooming by the stream perfumes sweeter than a whole pasture of blossoms.

The two lovers had now tasted each other and moved rashly into the other's arms as soon as they found a moment alone. The King held her so tightly that her ermine coat engulphed him.

That evening, the moon made it seem as bright as the day. The spring breeze filled the air with perfume. The singing birds made beautiful music. The King was sitting on his throne. His love for Shirin shined from his heart in such a way that he no longer need any candle or light. The breeze was bringing the message from Parviz, "Will there be another night better than tonight? Can we be happier than we are now? Why should we be away from each other? In such beautiful weather, why aren't we laughing?

"Every day is not spring and every hour is not one in which we capture our prey." His thought was with Shirin as he sat on his throne looking at Shah-Pour who stood before him and, on his other side, Shirin was like the Sun of pagan worshipers, circled by her ten beautiful friends. When they all drank enough wine to make their cheeks red, the King asked each one to tell a story. After every one of those ten beauties had told a story, it was Shah-Pour's turn.

"Shirin was honey in a cup, Parviz became her oil; together they made such a delicious cookie, and I am the saffron yellow of that cookie," he said. Then he gave them a prayer in Pahlavi and said, "I hope both of you shine in the world but do not live without each other."

When it was Shirin's turn, she made the weather full of perfume and the desert full of sugar. She said, "My heart was without love, and I had no lover when Shah-Pour came to fix the problem. Although our destiny was set, he was the one to make me fall in love with my King."

When it was Parviz's turn, he said, "There was a lion in the meadow. There was an elk who had a house in the lion's way. The elk put a chain around the lion's neck. I am that lion who Shirin, on the hunting trip, put the chain of her hairs on my neck. If I am not with her, I will die like a candle snuffed out by the wind. If she is with me, I will be able to defeat the fiercest of lions."

The joy in Shirin's heart was evident when she heard such sweet talk. She filled the cup with wine, gave it to Parviz and said, "Cheers, cheers. Drink this sweet wine with cheers. Forget everyone except Shirin."

The King drank the wine and was delighted at being with his lover. He said, "I want this night to linger forever, and I don't wish to see daylight in the sky. I want to be with you alone and tell you how much I love you. My heart is boiling for your love; I drink this delicious wine in the memory of your lips." He drank the wine and kissed her lips.

It was the norm to stay up late at night and Parviz's face was sweaty from the heat. He wondered how he could find Shirin drunk and sleep with her. There was no opportunity for him, though. His yearning heart wanted her all night until dawn.

When the sun sprayed its golden rays on the darkness of the night, the sun and the moon rode Golgoon and Shabdiz toward the jungle for hunting. They went from Moghan toward Shahrood. They made a city with wine and music. Sometimes they went toward the river and hunted both birds and fish. Sometimes they went to Mandoor Dasht and killed deer and goor (zebra). That was the way they spent their days; sometimes they went hunting, sometimes they had fun drinking and playing. During the nights, the King's maiden along with the other maids would sit all around him. The doves numerous, but the royal falcon was only one. Everyone drank for Parviz's health, and they were as happy as the birds. There was no night without music and songs. They never were without wine and chalice. Theirs was the garden of youth with wine and their lover. There was nothing better.

They watched the flowers and gardens, drank from each other's hands, and held each other tight like ivy to the elm tree. Sometimes he held her in his arms, and sometimes he put pansies in her hair. Sometimes they told each other their secrets. And sometimes they spoke of the sadness of being apart.

One day they all went hunting very early in the morning. They ran around for several hours and were tired. They rested at midday under tall trees by the river. They had their lunch with the sound of the falling water and singing birds, then wine and music followed. After several cups of wine passed around the group, the friends fell asleep one after another due to the tiring morning activities and the night's lack of sleep. Parviz looked around; he and Shirin were still awake. He smiled at her and got up and said, "Let's walk before we fall asleep too."

Shirin followed. A few yards away, he stopped. The surrounding scenery was magnificent. Wildflowers surrounded the tall waterfall at whose foot they stood. The flowering trees made a natural canopy and the green grass covered the ground like a soft bed. He pulled her into his arms and kissed her lips; he was hot and lustful. He said, "I love you so much that I will do whatever you want me to do like a slave who obeys his master. Whatever occurred in my life before, does not matter. Today is a new day and a new life. There is no one here except me and you, so now let's complete our fun. Just for one hour be mine, you will see that is the best hour of your life. We need to take advantage of our youth otherwise, we will get old without tasting joy. You are like a businessman with hundreds of kilos of sugar. What happens if you close the door for being stingy?"

Shirin told him, "Oh, my King, it is not okay for me who is like dust to sit on the same throne with the shining King. If I say no to you, it is because we are hot and drunk. When we get sober, the King will have as much sugar as he desires."

She tried to avoid getting too close to him in the hope of having him forever, but her heart was beating so hard, and inside she was more anxious than he to melt into his arms. Her face was red and her breathing rapid. She was saying no, but her whole body was signaling him that she wanted what he wanted.

Parviz laughed and started to kiss her. She turned her back to leave. Parviz held her tight and said, "Where are you going? You drank the same wine that I drank but how come you are sober and I am drunk? For me just kissing you is enough, you can stop me from kissing too if you want. However, I am so hot with your love that I will burn to death. I am afraid that tomorrow you will be sorrowful that you killed a lover like me. In that case, you will pay for my blood since the lover's blood never dies. If you do not want me to kiss your lips, then tell me what to kiss, your sleeves, your dress? If you kiss me, you will get ten back. What business deal is better than that? I will hug you like water surrounding rock; you have my soul so how can I hurt my own heart? You buy my heart, and I will sell my soul. You become a cupbearer so I can drink the wine. I will kiss you all over."

He held her and caressed her face. "You give a kiss, and I will count it. Let's have fun today since we know not what happens tomorrow. Do not play with that smooth hair of yours. Play with me, take care of me. My sweet spring, you are sweeter than life. It is so nice to hold you like my own soul. If I kiss your lips or your feet, they are sweeter than sugar everywhere I kiss. All over you are sweet, it is no wonder that they called you Shirin."

"Oh, my King, you are a fire now, and I will become smoke. In the market of love, being with you is a most joyful thing in the world, but you know one cannot play backgammon alone. We cannot live for fun. We both have a good reputation, and there is no reason to change that. Let's not shame ourselves. I am a sweet tree which has both cookies and sherbet. Drink the sherbet right now and you will have the cookies if you wait. Have you not heard that people who eat too much stay sick forever?"

Parviz started kissing her again and said, "Oh my moon, stop this nonsense, I came all this way to find you, and now that your hair is in my hand I am dying; being with you is all I want from the world. If you go away, I will be without my flower. If I am not with you, I will be full of despair." Then he held her tightly and started nudging her toward the bedding of the grass under their feet.

She tried to get away, but he gripped her so she could not squirm loose. She said, "Do not be so hot, the flower which gets hot does not perfume."

However, he did not listen to what she said. He unbuttoned her shirt and started kissing her breasts. A shiver of pleasure spread through her body which only increased his aggression. All of a sudden, she remembered her aunt's advice and pictured the beautiful women of the court. *What should I do? How can I stop him?*

Parviz was on top of her now. She said, "You cannot get the treasure without working for it. You must first find your Kingdom, and then you can have me."

Parviz stopped moving. He loosened his grip on her body.

"If you stay with me I am afraid you will not get your Kingdom back and even if you do who am I then; the forgotten one? This country is an old one, and it is beautiful in your hands, but it is a shameful place when it's in the hands of the others. The world belongs to those who work hard."

He stood up and pulled her to her feet. The anger in his heart boiled. He could not believe what she was telling him. *Was it true that she only loved him as a King?*

Shirin, who was so happy for stopping him, didn't notice his anger. "You cannot be a King and sit still. You are young and are like a lion. Go and kill that Hindu who has stolen your throne. Sometimes you get what you want with a sword and sometimes with a cup of wine. If you raise your sword, all over the country people will join your army. I will help too. I will send a prayer for your victory."

They were walking back towards where they had left their friends when his boiling anger started to flow. "Goodbye, my dear. I will go either to the sea or into the fire. It was your love that left me without a crown. If it wasn't for your love in my head, I would not be without my crown now. You first gave me wine and made me drunk, now that I am drunk you tell me to get up and fight with those who did not drink?

"I will get up all right, but first, I have to pull myself from the well you led me to. I am going away. I will listen to your advice and will try no matter what happens. You made me aware of my life, with good intention or not. In the beginning, I was such a lucky man with the crown and throne. You have made me a refugee in the world. If it were not for your love, what wind would have brought me to this soil?" Then he jumped on the back of Shabdiz and ordered his men, awoken by his noise, to leave the hunting place.

Shirin was stunned at his reaction. She dared not say anything before he disappeared in the dust of the road. She felt empty inside. The happiness and excitement of his arm were replaced with loneliness and regret.

Husrō-Parviz went back to his camp and told his men to start packing. A loyal soldier of his came to the camp in a hurry and asked to see the King. Parviz, who was supervising the move, let him approach.

The soldier bowed and said, "Long live the King. I came to tell you of the vast army Bahram has gathered to chase and capture or kill you."

"Where are they now? How many days do we have?"

"They are approximately two weeks away. I came without stopping when I heard."

"Thank you, my friend. You came in time, and hopefully we will be far away when they arrive. We will thank you if I stay alive and return."

He bowed and said, "Long live King Parviz, I am honored to give my life for my King. My best reward is your well-being."

His heart full of sadness from Shirin, Parviz started north to follow his father's advice and get help from the Romans. They took the road from Anglon toward the Roman capital.

CHAPTER 24

Shirin in Her Loneliness

Shirin could not think clearly for some time. She asked herself many questions. *Should I go after him and apologize? Apologize for what? What did I say to make him so mad? Oh, my God. It was such a pleasant moment in his arms, why did I spoil such a magnificent moment?*

An hour after his departure she ordered her companions to pack and go toward Parviz's camp. When they got there, they saw an empty space and the remains of the fire scattered about, the ashes still smoldering.

She went to her castle, closed the door, and let her tears wash her face. *I miss him so much only a few hours after he's left, how I can tolerate a lifetime without him?* She was depressed and unhappy, so she barred her door to all her friends and did not leave her castle.

Days passed, and the more her friends tried to cheer her up the less they could do. They went to her aunt, Mahin-Bano, and told her about the situation.

Mahin-Bano went to Shirin's castle. She found her niece who was devestated, her skin a sickly yellow, and her eyes red. Shirin bowed and said, "Long live my Queen aunt, Mahin. Welcome to this humble house."

Mahin-Bano took her in her arms and said, "My dear sweet Shirin. I do not want to see you sad. I have heard you have locked yourself in your house and did not go out or do anything."

Shirin's tears flowed like the rain, and she said, "Oh I don't know what to do with this sadness inside me."

"Let's sit and talk," her aunt said, holding her arms. "What happened and what is the cause of your sorrow?"

Shirin looked up at her with wide eyes and said, "I made him leave, and I miss him so much."

Mahin-Bano scowled. "Who? King Parviz?"

Shirin's tear increased, and she said, "He wanted me so badly, and I told him he should get his crown back before I could be with him. I just wanted him to marry me. But instead I made him mad, and he left without even kissing me goodbye. I am regretting what I said."

Mahin-Bano started caressing her hair. "Oh, my sweet, do not blame yourself since you saved his life with your words. You made him leave all right, and that was the best thing otherwise you would mourn his death if you were not killed yourself."

Shirin looked at her aunt with confusion and asked, "What are you talking about?"

"Well, a large army has just come to town in search of Parviz and when they found that he had gone, they went after him. If you did not say anything, both of you would have been so immersed in your playing, hunting, and lovemaking that he would not have noticed the danger looming over him. If he were here today, he certainly would be killed, and you might be too."

Shirin said, "No, he is so strong, and he would fight them. We could help."

"No, my dear, he is strong but that powerful army was too big for him, or even us, to fight. I am glad that he left. He will not forget your love, my dear. If he stays alive, he will come back to

86

you. I am sure of it. My dove, I could see the intense love he had for you. You are going to be the Shah of this land soon, and you need to come to the governor's office with me to learn. It will keep you busy until your love comes back and unites with you. Then he will have his throne back."

The soothing voice of her aunt's advice made her calm down, so she obeyed and went to the governor's office to observe her aunt's duties and learn how to govern. She became busy, and although deep inside she felt a heavy sadness for being apart from her first and only love, she was calmer and hopeful for his return. Several months later her aunt became ill and left her in charge.

None of the medical treatments Mahin-Bano received worked, and she died and left Shirin without a relative in the world.

This loss was very hard on Shirin, who had first experienced the loss of her love and now the loss of her aunt, the woman who was like both her mother and father. However, she was now the Shah of Armenia and was supposed to be strong. She governed the state as the best governor to date, and everyone was happy with her style of rule.

A year passed. The state business kept her so busy that she hardly had time for self-pity when one day a guard came in and said, "A Persian man called Shah-Pour wants to see you."

Shirin's heart sped its beat. *Is he coming to tell me about him, is it possible that Parviz is sending him to reunite with me?* She tried to get ahold of her emotion and said, "Oh yes, send him in, I need to speak with him alone."

Everyone left the room when Shah-Pour entered. He bowed and said, "Long live the Queen of beauty, the Shah of Armenia."

"Get up my friend. Welcome to our land, what news do you bring us?"

"I hope my Queen is healthy, I have good news and am sorry to say that I am going to give you bad news too."

Shirin's heart squeezed tight, and a pain of sadness overcame her mood. She asked with worry, "Is it Parviz? Did something happen to him?"

"My Lady, he is okay, and that is my good news. When we left Armenia, we advanced to Dara castle. We were resting when Bahram's army surrounded us. We did not know what to do. They knew that we could not stay in the castle forever so the King asked everyone "What should we do?"

"His Uncle Gostham told the King, "Give me your clothing and leave the castle in the middle of the night. I will take care of the rest."

"We did as he suggested. Apparently, he put on the King's clothing and went to the roof. Braham and his army believed it was our King because of their resemblance from a distance. The next day, he put on his clothing and went on the roof and told them that the King was tired and would leave the castle after he rested for a few days. He appeared again on the roof the next day and said, "Our King is praying today and will surrender himself tomorrow."

"By that time, we were on Roman soil, and Parviz had sent a message to the Roman Empire for assistance. Caesar agreed to help him. He gave him money and a great army to bring back to Iran.

"After Gostham had gone out of the castle and given himself up, they discovered that Parviz had fled. He was imprisoned, however, he talked to his guard and promised him a big reward after Parviz came back. So Gostham was freed, and when we got back to Iran, he joined us as we marched to the war with Bahram.""

Shirin asked impatiently "So what happened with the war?"

"Well, with God's help and the Roman's army and money, we won the battle, and Bahram fled to China. Parviz is our great King now without any rival."

Shirin's lips parted with the most beautiful smile, and she said, "Oh thanks be to God. Then she paused and asked, "What is your bad news?"

Shah-Pour bent down his head and stayed quiet for a while. Then when Shirin looked at him with inquiring eyes, he said, "Our King had to marry Princess Maryam, Caesar's daughter. He also had to give up Armenia, so there would be no longer war between Iran and Rome."

Shah-Pour's words were like a hammer hitting her head. *He married! Does he prefer someone else as his bride over me?*

She did not understand why he kept talking. "You know for several hundred years we've had a fight with the Romans over Dara's Castle."

"What? What about Dara's Castle?"

"Well, My Lady, as I was saying, Caesar Maurice received much of Persian Armenia and western Georgia and was granted abolition of the subsidies which had formerly been paid to the Sasanians. Armenia was given to Rome for their help, and from now on there will be a long peace between the two countries."

"He did what? To gain his throne back, he gave up one of Iran's states to the Romans? Wow, to me, that is treason."

"Oh, My Lady, you are angry, but you should not accuse our King of treason. You know better than anyone how much he loves his country. His ancestors have kept this country as one of the greatest Empires of the world, and he will make it more prosperous than ever."

"He gave one of his states to an enemy, did he not?"

"Yes, My Lady, but by doing so, he saved the Persian Empire and prevented the bloodshed and destruction of the war which had loomed over his country for many years. He also was able to kick that Hindu out of the country as you wished!"

Shirin frowned and said, "You are right. It was my tongue

which pushed him to leave, but I did not imagine he would give up Armenia! Was it not enough to marry Princess Maryam? Does he hate me so much that he gave up my homeland?"

"My dear Lady, his decision was not an act of revenge. You know that the Romans had an eye on Armenia for a long time. They wanted it and asked for it as a condition for helping him with his army and coins."

"Yes, they contributed to destroying this land. Can you not see! They sent him a big army and placed spies in his court. He will not be able to move without her permission."

"My Lady, I do not think the King will obey the Romans the way you imagine it. It was just a way to bring an end to the long animosity between the two countries. Princess Maryam is a token of peace between our King and her father. I assure you if there is any aggression from Rome, she will be the one to suffer first. And since Caesar does not want any harm to his daughter, he will not make any attacks except those within their agreement."

Shirin shook her head and said, "Well you love him as much as I do except you do not see his faults, but I see them and still love him. From what you are telling me, then my job as a Shah of this land is ending since the Romans will send their governor and I will have to leave my homeland."

"Yes, Your Majesty that is what I imagine they will do."

"How long do I have to pack?"

"I do not know Your Majesty. I imagine as soon as the news of Bahram's defeat reaches the Roman Empire they will send a new governor. However, I estimate it will take at least a month for the news to reach them and send a new ruler."

"Well, then I have to get ready. Thank you for letting me know before they arrive so I wouldn't be surprised by their coming."

Shah-Pour bowed and said "Your Majesty, I am sorry that I am not the bearer of better news. But remember, no matter where you go I will be accompanying you and doing everything in my power to help in any way I can."

"Thank you Shah-Pour I appreciate your loyalty."

Over the next several days Shirin started to pack. She gave some money to the fire temple and the needy. Then she took all her belongings, money, coins and jewelry. She organized all her livestock: lambs, cows, horses, and camels. From those forty beauties, she took a few of them with her since they were always by her side sharing her sadness and happiness. She left, riding her favorite horse Golgoon, while Shah-Pour accompanied her.

Shirin and her companions turned east and south from Azerbaijan and Kurdistan, heading to Bakhtaran. She intended to find a place to settle down, and she found Bakhtaran to her liking.

Shah-Pour realized that Shirin was going to stay in that region and was in search of a person to build her a castle. He asked her if he might take a few weeks off and visit his relatives. Shirin granted his wish, and so Shah-Pour left.

CHAPTER 25

Shah-Hanshah Husrō-Parviz

Husrō-Parviz defeated Bahram and got his throne back. Every one of the governors from all over the Persian Empire sent their congratulations and gifts. However, all the glories of his new Kingdom did nothing to lessen the pain of being away from Shirin. While he was fighting Bahram he had not thought that much about her, but now that he was a victorious King his forgotten love started burning him from inside. He could not throw away his pain nor could he call on the person who was causing the pain. His wife was Maryam, but he wished it was Shirin instead.

He was able to have fun but never any deep satisfaction. Although he had the Kingdom and all its treasure, he was sad for not having his love by his side. Sometimes he drank the bitter wine and sometimes he made the wine with his tears. He would ask himself, *what do you want from life, Love or a Kingdom? There is no way you can have both. You have to choose one or the other. If I were in love with being a King, I would be happy now. When did my luck die out? The day I woke up without any true lover. Oh, what happened to the time I was sitting between all those beautiful women and had that Queen of beauty in my arms? Where is my Shirin with her sweet words? What happened to all those nights that we did not sleep and stayed up to tell the stories? Oh, where is that beautiful flower whose lips I kissed so many times? When I was drunk, I sat by her and those times that I held her in my arms. Those stories that we told each other. Was it a dream or my imagination? The one I seek was spring, but a wind took her away from me.*

Then he started advising himself that being a King would be good for him. He had a duty to his country to be a King and govern his enormous Empire.

CHAPTER 26

The Birth of the Shah-Hanshah's Son

Excitement ran through the court when Maryam went into labor. The King was anxious to see his first born, too. He was overjoyed when he was told his firstborn was a boy. He went to see his Queen and the baby. The boy was healthy and adorable. They named him Qobād, in memory of his great-grandfather, and gave the nickname Shiruya.

The castle became light day and night, and music and song filled the air. Everyone was celebrating the birth of the Crown Prince. As was customary, Parviz asked his astronomers to see what the future would bring his newborn. Three nights after he was born the King admitted the astronomers into his chamber to hear the fate of his son.

The chief astronomer bowed and said "Shah-Hanshah be Javidan. We looked at the stars and are ready to tell you what we found."

Parviz smiled and said, "I am anxious to hear your findings."

"We hope that you will have a long life with more power and prosperity, but I am sorry to tell you we do not have good news for you. We see disturbances and riots when he reaches power. Your army will not praise him. He also will turn away from God and will do unbelievable things. We cannot tell you more."

The King was mad and disturbed at the same time. "Go and look again. If you see anything else, let me know. However, do not say a word about this to any of the Persian nobles."

They bowed and said, "Your Majesty, we will do what you told us and will guard this secret with our souls." Then they gave him the tomar wrapped in yellow silk.

"You have my permission to depart now." They bowed and left the King with sadness. He gave the tomar to his treasurer to be kept in the safe. For a week, he sat alone thinking. *What should I do? He is such a beautiful baby, should I believe their prediction and kill my son?* These thoughts attacked him day and night. He did not drink or go hunting or listen to his favorite musicians.

People noticed and grew worried. The elders went and saw the Mobed and asked him, "We want to know what is wrong with the King and why he is refusing to see us?"

Mobed went to the Shah's chamber and told him everything he'd heard from the elders. Parviz said, "I grew depressed from what the astronomers warned me about my newborn son. I did not read the tomar that they wrote for him, but you can read it and tell me what to do." Then he told the guardian of his treasure, "Go and get the yellow silk, inside it, is a tomar and let the Mobed read it."

When his Mobed read the written words, he was silent for a few minutes then he said, "God knows more than anyone else. No one can change destiny by crying. It is not wise to be unhappy. Do not talk or think about what they say, be happy and be sure nothing bad will happen soon."

After the Mobed had left, Parviz decided to change his behavior. He wrote a letter to Caesar and told him, "Dear Emperor, congratulations are due since Maryam bore a son. Never has anyone seen such a beautiful baby. I hope he gains knowledge and glory and learns generosity. I am happy, and I know you deserve happiness since being a King suits you."

When Parviz's letter reached Rome, there was a ceremony and party for Shiruya with singing, praying and dancing. Then Caesar sent many gifts to welcome the birth of his grandson.

CHAPTER 27

Shah-Pour Visits with Parviz

Shah-Pour was sent by Parviz to see Shirin's reaction and to be sure she was ok and did not need for anything. He was meant to report her well-being to the King since both lovers trusted him. It was an easy task.

After he had left Shirin, he went to Tisfoon and was greeted by Parviz. The King held a private meeting to see how his lover was doing.

Shah-Pour bowed and said, "Long live the King of Kings. King of seven states, Parviz."

"Oh, Shah-Pour get up now. I was waiting to hear from you. I've missed talking to you so much."

Shah-Pour bowed and said, "I hope my King is happy. I am honored to know my worthless being has the attention of our great King. What is wrong Your Majesty? I trace sadness in your talk. You are now our great and victorious King and should be triumphant."

"Oh, Shah-Pour you have to be the one who knows my problems. Tell me now, what is the benefit of having a golden chain on my feet if I want to go to the garden? I cannot cut this chain from my feet, and I cannot fly to the orchard with this chain. Although, my treasure has been increased, without Shirin my pain has also increased."

Shah-Pour said, "I am sorry Majesty, all I can say is that she is unhappier than you and regrets any word she said that day."

Parviz's lips opened up to smile like a bud opening to sunshine. "You saw her then. How is she doing?"

"I am sorry to tell you that she is not well. She regrets what she said but is very upset with your actions. She thinks you sold her and her country and is very bitter, although she still weeps for losing you."

Parviz bent down his head and after a pause said, "I don't blame her. But she should know that my actions were the result of her demands. I was content to stay in one place and just have her. She told me I had to get my throne back. I got it back, but for a price. You should assure her that I did not want to hurt her and if I did, it was not intentional."

"I told her that, however, I do not think I was able to convince her."

"Where is she now?"

"She was settling down in Bakhtaran when I left. She liked that site and was looking to build her castle there."

When Parviz heard that his lover was closer than he thought, he felt a ray of hope in his heart. He was afraid of Maryam since day and night she observed his actions. He knew that he could not bring Shirin to his castle, and he was too busy to go where she was. So, he decided to forget her. However, the harder he tried, the less successful he was in forgetting. Day and night, he thought of her. He called Barbed, his musician, to play. He stayed up late drinking wine with his old friend and confidant. But rather than forget her, an idea grew in his head.

Bringing the deposed Shahs to the capital was customary.

What if he could get permission from Maryam? He went home and asked her.

"You know my dear that I had to give up Armenia in exchange for your father's help. Well, the Shah of Armenia is now without any home and is wandering the desert, trying to find a place to live."

The bitterness of jealousy entered Maryam's heart when she heard of the Shah of Armani. She had heard stories about the heated love affair between the two. However, she decided to listen.

Parviz continued, "It is better that she be away from me, and I am not the least interested in seeing her. However, she was one our best Shahs, and she lost her position due to our agreement with your father, not for any fault we saw in her. If you permit me, I will make a castle for her and let her live with her companions. I promise that I will not see her and if I do, will fill my eyes with fire."

Maryam answered him, "Oh my darling your glory covers the world like stars. However, if Shirin's name is a sweet meat, you will not get to eat it. She will use all her tricks and magics to deceive you. She will trick you and make you send me away. You will love her, and I will mourn for you. I know her incantations. I've heard about these kinds of betrayals.

"What have you seen from that unbeliever? All you have had from her was trouble. No, I will not let that happen. I swear to Caesar's Crown and the King of King's throne. If Shirin gets close to this city, I will take the black rope and kill myself, so my life becomes free of your torment."

King-Parviz told her, "Calm down. It was not my intention to make you unhappy. It is just that I thought she, like any other King, should benefit from our respect and kindness. Since you do not permit that, I understand."

Then he changed the subject and asked her about their new-born baby, who was only a month old. He loved that little boy and was somber since the forecasters had told him about the child's future. He hid that forecast from his wife, but it added to his inner turmoil.

So, his life passed like this, keeping secrets, being a good husband and sitting King. He was also in love secretly about which only Shah-Pour knew. He saw Shah-Pour often and asked about Shirin. Shah-Pour did not hide his visits to the King from Shirin and told her everything that the King said. Shirin wondered how he could live without her.

CHAPTER 28

King Parviz Asks Shah-Pour to See Shirin

One day Shah-Pour arrived to visit the King and went in and as was his habit bowed and kissed Parviz's hand. "Long live the King of Kings. I do not want to see you so sad. What is bothering you again?"

"What else? It is a pain that only you are aware of. I cannot understand how long I have to wait to see her. Can you please make Shirin come here one night without anyone noticing? I cannot have her here openly since I am afraid that Maryam will kill herself if she knows that I am in touch with Shirin, and I will have a big war in front of me. For my country and my Kingdom, I cannot do anything openly with Shirin. However, I will take care of her as nobody else can. I only want to see her once. Can you bring her here secretly?"

He bowed his head and said, "I will try my best, and I will give your message to her as soon as possible."

Shah-Pour rode as fast as he could to where Shirin was camping. Shirin was sitting in her luxurious tent with several of her friends and workers. They were in the middle of a discussion when

Shah-Pour arrived. As soon as Shirin saw him, she signaled him to come in and responding to his greeting said, "Come Shah-Pour. We need to get your advice about something."

Shah-Pour bowed and said, "I have an important message for you that cannot wait. If you permit me to talk to you in private, I'll be honored."

Shirin was surprised, and at the same time curious, so she hastened her companions to leave. When there was nobody but her and Shah-Pour, she said, "Ok my friend, tell me what your message is and from whom you bring it?"

Shah-Pour bowed again and said, "Your Majesty knows my love for both you and my grandmaster the King of Kings, Parviz. It is with utmost pleasure I tell you that he sends me to say his love for you is as fresh as when he left you, and he is miserable without you. However, his sword is dull in front of Maryam. He is so cautious because of his agreement with Caesar."

Shirin, who was listening to him, frowned and said, "This is not news. You told me you have a message for me from him. This is what you have been telling me since we left my homeland."

Shah-Pour said, "No I am saying what he asked me to tell you. That he loves you dearly and ..."

Shirin interrupted him impatiently and said, "Oh I see, now he remembers he loves me? What is he going to do with that now?"

"Well, it is up to you if you want to be with him or not. He wants you to go to the capital with me. You two can see each other in private and end these unhappy feeling you both have."

Shirin immediately grew angry. She started shouting at Shah-Pour. "If you are not ashamed of yourself, be ashamed of your God. Stop talking, since your suggestion gives me a big headache. I did not expect this from you! I hope God takes you away from this ugly business, and you learn a lesson from your wisdom. He took away my crown and now he wants to take away my life?

Look, what am I doing here? I am getting used to being sad. That lover of mine, he did not even send a letter to greet me. It is not right for a woman like me to fight a King of Kings. It was the bad luck that he came to me, and now I have tears in my heart. I was picking flowers; now I am surrounded by thorns. I cannot complain to anyone but myself, though. I said that he is my soul and my world. He took away my world and now he wants my soul! I cannot deny my own fault. The scale has two ends, not one. You put the grain in one and money in another. However, the scale that Parviz gave me has only one end, and that is full of grain. What did he do for me except give me pain both inside and out? I am alive, and he is with another lover. I have suffered so much from him. Although I always told him true, he still is not honest. How can I believe his claim when he wants to destroy the reputation of a woman like me?

"There is no space for reconciliation. I am so mad at Parviz for all he gives me is a pain in my heart. I am not going anywhere near him even if it is my destiny. I am the one who is crying day and night. You cannot teach a crying person how to not moan. I have always been happy with his memory, but he didn't remember me at all.

"Usually, the same species fly together, the dove with dove, and the falcon with the falcon. You cannot mix water and fire together. Since I've been away from him so long, I will not be afraid of being alone longer. I am not the kind of bird that anyone can put in a cage, nor can any falcon capture me. If Maryam is a Princess, then know I was a Queen. I cannot forget the bitter fact that I am miserable, and Maryam is happy.

"Well, it was destiny I guess. I made a joke, and he thought I was requesting it. I lied, and he thought it was the truth. I am not cursing him or wishing him anything bad. Although I am away from my treasure and my country, I am free. Therefore, he cannot order me to go and be his mistress."

Shirin was talking rapidly and walking back and forth in her spacious tent while Shah-Pour was quiet and listened without any emotion.

Shirin stopped and looked at him. She said, "If he told you he is madly in love with me tell him I do not believe a word he says. If he asks when he gets to see Shirin? Tell him to break the fast with Maryam and be content. If he says I will hold her in my arms, say he should forget this desire." After speaking, her anger cooled a bit.

She sat on the throne and with a calmer voice said, "My friend when you see the King give him my regards and my message. Tell him I said, "What happened to that sweet talk of yours? I thought you would not leave me and would not fall for any idol but me. Well, now you have made me understand that I was wrong. You let my enemy enter your heart. Remember Shirin's sadness. Do not want me abashedly. I am as noble as you so can't treat me like a slave. Why are you looking at me like a servant when I am your equal in nobility?

"When you were a runaway, you basked in my sight, but when became a King you closed your eyes to my love. When no one was your friend I was your lover, but now you do not want anything to do with me. Now that you have a flower from the Roman gardens do not destroy the Armenian Queen. Let me be in this sadness to worship my God. Although I am miserable, I want all the sorrow and agony away from my King."

Shah-Pour listened to Shirin's speech then bowed and said, "What you say is right, and you know better than me what is good for you."

Shirin said, "Now that you agree with me, go out and ask the others to come in so we can tend to important issues."

Shah-Pour called those who were in the tent back, not knowing what was going to be discussed. He saw the anger in Shirin's eyes and was nervous since he did not want to lose her trust. He was genuinely fond of her and enjoyed being in her service, but beyond that, he was Parviz's agent in making sure Shirin received what she sought. Although what Shirin needed was to talk to him about their King and hear that he still loved her. He had not anticipated the anger he saw when he gave her the King's proposal message. He wondered what his relationship with Shirin would be after this outburst of emotion. Everyone came in and looked at Shirin, who was sitting as calm as she could wearing the same green dress and smiling as usual.

She began elegantly, "As you know, we need to settle down somewhere since our beloved King gave our land to our enemies." She looked at Shah-Pour pointedly and continued. I like this place and want to settle down here. I need an engineer to build me a castle and I want all of you to search for the person who can do the job. I know some of you have looked around and have not found anyone with the reputation to do it. But I want you to search further and find him. The winter will be here soon, and we cannot live in these tents for long.

Everyone was quiet, but Shah-Pour felt tickled; he could get her attention and trust sooner than he thought. He got up, bowed and said, "If My Lady gives me permission."

Shirin grinned and said, "Oh Shah-Pour, go ahead and let us know what we should do?"

Shah-Pour bowed again and said, "When I was going to painting school I got to know an architect and civil engineer who could build from rock the most beautiful castles. His name is Farhad."

Shirin's face opened up like a new bud in the spring. "So, you think he can manage to build my castle in this beautiful land?"

Shah-Pour bowed again." Yes, My Lady, if there is one person to build the castle that you want, it is Farhad."

"Ok, can you find him or give the direction for my servants to go and fetch him?"

"Of course, My Lady, however, I need to see the King first, and on my way back I will make Farhad come with me to Your Majesty's court."

Shirin smiled. "Oh, of course, you cannot keep the King of Kings waiting too long."

Shah-Pour bowed and said, "My first loyalty is to Your Majesty, only Ecbatana is on my way to Tisfoon and ..."

Shirin interrupted him and said, "I did not mean to doubt your loyalty. I don't care where you stop on your way to this engineer. Just hurry up and leave as soon as you can."

Shah-Pour bowed and said, "I will leave at once, and after meeting with the King I will go to Ecbatana. I saw him last in there, where he was building the governor's house. If my calculation is right, he should be at the tail end of this project and can come with me on my way back."

Shirin gave him her beautiful smile and said, "Excellent," then clapped her hands, and the meeting was adjourned. Shah-Pour went to his tent to get ready for his trip to Tisfoon.

When he was done, he went to the stable to saddle his horse. He saw that Shirin had too mounted her horse and, along with three companions, seemed to be going hunting.

However, he knew that in truth she was going for a ride to clear her mind since she always started her hunting trips very early in the morning. Shah-Pour knew Shirin very well. She was madly in love with the King and rejecting his offer to be with him had been very hard for her. He could see that her mind was fighting with her heart. Her pride against her love. If it were not for her noble upbringing, she would not have been able to resist the temptation. He loved them both and was so sad that the circumstances put such distance between the two of them.

He looked at the four slender, beautiful women riding stallions leaving the camp. He shook his head and he and his horse rode off in the opposite direction.

CHAPTER 29

———◦———◦———

Shah-Pour in Tisfoon

It was late at night when Shah-Pour got to Tisfoon and went to Parviz's castle. He showed his pass and went inside. When the guard told the King who was asking permission to enter, the King was half drunk listening to his musicians. He beckoned them to leave him and told the guard to let Shah-Pour in. His heart was murmuring in anticipation of hearing what his beloved Shirin has told his messenger.

The musicians and the other audiences left the room. Shah-Pour entered and bowed. "Long live the King of Kings."

The King stood and said, "It is so nice to see you. Come and sit next to me please." He beckoned him forward. He obliged nervously.

The King sensed his nervousness said in a calm voice, "Tell me what has my love said that disturbed you so much?"

Shah-Pour sighed in relief. "I hope my King is in perfect health and will rule over more land than any other Kings have ruled. Princess Shirin is in excellent health and is still is very much in love with you. However, she is too proud to accept your proposal."

The King of Kings got up and paced the room." Please tell me everything she said, even the part that is not to my liking. I want to hear all of it."

Shah-Pour, who had risen when the King stood, said "Your Majesty I do not wish to burden you with unnecessary details. To summarize it, she admitted that she loves you very much, but she cannot accept your proposal. She said that she was kidding you when she encouraged you to get your crown back. Therefore, she is to blame for your marriage, and she is doomed to mourn this separation as long as she lives."

The King sat down, held his head in his hands, and said, "You know my dear friend, you are the only one who knows how miserable I am here in this palace. Sometimes I wish I were an ordinary man who married his sweetheart and lived happily ever after. I am not sure ... even if she had not enticed me to get my crown back, I might still stay. I cannot abandon my responsibility to my homeland as a King. But I cannot clear my mind either. I want her so badly."

Shah-Pour shook his head in agreement and said, "I understand Your Majesty, but I am afraid she does not understand. She is very bitter for both your marriage and your consent with the Romans. She said, "If Maryam is a Princess know I was a Shah. I cannot forget the bitter fact that I am miserable, and Maryam is happy. Well, it was destiny I guess. I am not cursing him or wishing him anything bad. Although I am away from my treasure and my country, I am free. Therefore, he cannot order me to go and be his mistress.""

The King laughed bitterly and said, "Well she is right; destiny separated us and made us miserable."

Shah-Pour said, "You do not need to suffer Your Majesty. You have your Kingdom and your Queen. You need to enjoy your life and your fortune. When you lost your father, you were upset, but you came to accept it. Just imagine you lost Princess Shirin as well and get over your sadness."

He clapped his hands and said, "Wise advice. But have you

not heard that the dead person's soil is cold? In other words, it is easier to forget the loss of a loved one to the angel of death than to circumstances."

Shah-Pour said in a fatherly tone, "My dear Majesty our happiness or sadness lies in our head. If we think about those less fortunate than us, then we will feel fortunate. You have everything any person can wish for. You are young and healthy, ruling over vast lands of the Persian Empire, and have a Queen with a child. If you want my humble opinion, you should forget about Shirin and enjoy your life and your Kingdom."

"Thank you for your frankness. You are right, I will try to follow your advice. However, I think you have come a long way and are tired. Go and rest. Are you going back to Shirin's camp?"

Shah-Pour bowed and said, "Long live Shah-Hanshah. I am going to Ecbatana to fetch an engineer called Farhad to build Her Majesty a castle."

The King frowned. "So, is she planning to stay in that area for the rest of her life?"

"Yes, Your Majesty, she likes the weather there, since it is similar to the climate in Armenia."

"You will let me know if she needs anything. Does she need any money to build the palace?"

"Of course, Your Majesty, I will let you know. You know that she is a wealthy woman so right now what she needs is not money."

"Farewell then. Have a restful night and have a safe trip tomorrow."

Shah-Pour bowed and said, "Long live my King of Kings."

For several minutes after Shah-Pour left, Parviz sat drowned in his thoughts. *She is still in love with me but for how long? Will I ever be able to see her? What if she falls in love with another man?* He shook his head and got up to go to his bed.

CHAPTER 30

Farhad Falls in Love

Shah-Pour found Farhad and asked if he would go to Princess Shirin's camp to build a castle for her. Farhad rode with Shah-Pour to the location. When they arrived, it was late at night, so they went to sleep and asked for admission in the morning.

The engineer was tall with wide shoulders. He was stronger than two elephants. They were guided to the tent and were placed near the Princess's seat. Farhad was talking with Shah-Pour when sweet laughter spread the air and in came the magnificent, beautiful woman. She was dressed in orange silk and looked like an angel of beauty. She sat on her throne and, with her sweet tongue, welcomed both Shah-Pour and Farhad. Shah-Pour and Farhad rose and bowed in respect, and Shah-Pour introduced Farhad to Shirin.

She said with the most alluring voice, "Sit down, won't you please? How was your trip? I hope it did not tire you overly much."

Farhad sat mutely, staring at the beautiful lady sitting on the throne. He could not accept that she was indeed a real woman and not a dream. Shah-Pour looked at him with astonishment and answered Princess Shirin. "Long live My Lady. We had a beautiful trip back here. The weather was good, and we enjoyed our trip, Your Majesty."

"I am glad to hear that. Everything was fine in the capital I assume?"

"Yes, Your Majesty all was okay. Our King sends his regards and said to let him know if you need anything."

Shirin fell silence for a minute then she recovered from her internal disturbance and said, "You should thank our King. He should know that all we need from him is to be healthy and keep our country intact."

Then she looked at Farhad and said, "I hope Shah-Pour has told you that I need a palace here for my residence. I also love to drink milk. However, here we have so many beautiful nerium oleander shrubs that I must keep my animals away from them on the top of the mountain. The distance of the creatures from here is too far. To be able to obtain the milk every day, someone has to climb the Rogue Mountain and carry a large amount of milk for both my drinking consumption and my milk bath. I want you to make a waterway through rocks where my shepherds can send the milk through so we can have fresh milk every day. Can you make that possible?"

Farhad could hear her but did not understand a word. Her beauty and her sweet talk made him speechless, so he just shook his head in agreement and put his fingers on his eyes to show that he would obey every order.

Shirin gave him the most beautiful smile and got up. Everyone stood until Shirin left the tent.

Farhad felt like he had just woken up from a pleasant dream. Then he realized that he was not dreaming. *What happened? I don't remember what was said!*

He looked at the person next to him and asked, "Can you please repeat everything the Princess told me to do?"

The man called Homayoon frowned and said, "Didn't you hear her? You were sitting here just like me!"

"No, my dear friend. I am drunk and drunken men are deaf and blind. Please repeat what she wants."

Homayoon, who was amused, repeated Shirin's speech word for word. Farhad thanked him and started working right away. He gathered the necessary material and hired the helpers to begin the palace. He completed the work faster than anyone's expectations. When the castle was finished, he received his wages in gold.

Then Farhad started to cut the rocks for the waterway. His adze cut the hardest rocks and within a month he had created a marble waterway through the mountain rock. He formed a small pool at its bottom.

They took the news to the Princess that Farhad completed the waterway and the pool. She went to see it and was amused that it was so natural; no one would believe that it was built by humans and not nature. She said, "Wow, this is done so beautifully, I must thank him for doing such a marvelous job. Go and bring Farhad to the palace as soon as you can."

The maid bowed and left to fetch Farhad. Shirin was sitting on her throne when Farhad came in. He bowed and said, "A thousand applauses be upon the most beautiful Princess. I am at your service."

Shirin's sweet voice spread through the hall. "My dear Farhad, come, come and sit next to me." She pointed to the chair on her right.

Farhad obeyed and sat down, looking at Shirin with love and awe. He was madly in love with the beautiful Princess. He'd been warned though that she was in love with the mighty King of Kings of the Persian Empire, and even the Princes and Shahs did not dare to get close to her for that reason. However, he could not help dreaming. He was satisfied to see her now and then, but now that the project was finished he was worried he might no longer be able to see her.

Shirin broke his thoughts when she said with an excited voice. "You did such a good job that I do not know how to best appreciate your marvelous work of art." She had beautiful earrings in her ears which were very expensive. She took the earrings off and with an alluring voice said, "Take these and sell them. When I have more to give, I will pay you what you need."

Farhad took the earrings and said, "This beautiful jewelry is only worthy of you, I cannot possibly sell it to anyone. You already gave me more than my wages." Then he kissed the earrings and threw them at Shirin's feet. He bowed and left the hall.

Shirin, who was surprised by his behavior, looked around and asked. "What was that all about? Do you think it was not enough?"

Her close friend, Farangis, laughed and said, "Oh Your Majesty have you not heard? He is in love with you, and he sings love songs all day long."

Shirin frowned and said, "Since when? Does not he know my feelings?"

Homayoon, who repeated Shirin's request to Farhad the first day, asked permission to talk and when it was granted said, "He fell in love the first day he saw Your Majesty. He did not understand a word you were saying and asked me to repeat everything. He told me he was drunk. When I heard his songs, I told him that he was walking a thin line and was going to hurt himself. He said he was satisfied with just seeing you now and then from a distance."

Her lips smiled and with her eyebrow raised she said, "Well as long as he does not expect anything else he can sing love songs as long as his heart desires."

Farangis said with a sweet smile, "If you permit me, I would like to give my opinion My Lady."

Shirin sighed in agreement and motioned to go ahead.

Farangis said, "My Lady all of us need a companion. Farhad is the most handsome man I have ever seen. He is witty, talented and worthy of the most beautiful Princess."

Shirin frowned and said, "What are you suggesting?"

"Well My Lady, he is in love with you, and you are alone and unattached."

She looked at her friend angrily and said, "If you were not my best friend you would be dismissed. Stop this nonsense. The project is done, and I do not need him any longer." Farangis put her head down and bowed.

CHAPTER 31

Farhad's Pain for Shirin's Love

*F*arhad left Shirin and journeyed toward the desert. He was crying and singing love songs. He did not want to see his friends or his enemies. All he knew was the picture of Shirin in his heart. Life was hard, and he could not do anything about it. He ran up the mountain and across the desert to calm the fire in his soul. He cried sometimes and sang at other times. His tall figure was bending like a flower in the wind. He could not talk to anyone who would have sympathy for him. He knew what his pain was but did not know what his cure was. He neither had permission to send her a gift nor a close friend to send her a message.

His days passed in agony and his nights were mostly filled with tears. He would run long distances to free himself of the pain which was burning him from inside out. He thought about what Homayoon told him: "She is in love with the great King of Persia, and her love is not one-sided, he is in love with her too. Do not dig your own grave. Forget her. Otherwise, you will destroy yourself with a one-way love affair."

She is in love with him but is living alone here. If he loves her, why is he not here or why isn't she in the capital city? I don't understand it! Well, it is true that she does not love me. As kind as she has been, I have not seen the admiration of an independent woman in her eyes. But is it possible that gradually she might notice me as a lover instead of an employee?

He did not want to accept that his love was just a mirage. Farhad did not listen to people who warned him about his inner thoughts. He visited Princess Shirin once a week when she would accept his guests. He was satisfied with being close to her and seeing her from a distance. Then he would go back to the desert; he would run or walk all day and then would stop by the pool full of milk and drink from it. Since most of the time he could not sleep he would just walk around the pool imagining the Shirin bathing. The story of his love and infatuation spread around the world, and people started to talk about this one-way love affair.

CHAPTER 32

Farhad's Love Story Reaches Shah Parviz

ne night, the King was playing chess with one of his trusted friends called Rostam, and he asked, "Your Highness, have you heard the new love story in town?"

"No, whose love story?"

"Farhad's love story for Princess Shirin."

The King felt a butterfly in his heart. He knew this feeling would come whenever he heard her name. He frowned. The name Farhad rang in his ear, but he could not remember where he'd heard it. "Who is Farhad?"

Rostam did not notice the King's inner turmoil and answered in a calm voice, "Oh, he is the engineer who built her castle. He is falling madly in love with her. His story is all over town. He is so madly in love that he is running all over mountains and deserts. Day and night, he talks about her beautiful face. He says he is in love with her and sings love songs out loud. That is why his story is spreading all over. He is neither scared of the old or young nor is he afraid of the sword or dart."

The King asked indifferently "Does she know of his love? Is she responding in any way to encourage him?"

"She must be for his story is all over town. He goes to her palace once a week when she accepts visitors. He is happy to see her from a distance and hear her voice." Then he smiled. "No, if she encouraged him in any way he would not run all over the mountains like a madman!"

The King's mind was so disturbed that he lost the game. He glared at Rostam. "Well is he worthy of her? She is very particular when it comes to choosing a lover."

"From what I hear, he is very handsome and intelligent. Yes, he is worthy, if she gave him the time of day and he did not go mad,"

The King said, "Well enough of this crazy man. Let's go to bed, dear friend. Good night."

Rostam got up, bowed and said, "Good night, Your Majesty."

Husrō-Parviz could not go to sleep. The story disturbed him very badly. His love and lust for Shirin came back in force. Two nightingales sing better songs for one flower. If there are two demands for the same thing, then the price goes up. The fact that someone else was in love with his only love was both good and bad. On one hand, his heart was telling him: *See you are not alone feeling sadness from her love.*

But in the other hand, jealousy overwhelmed him, and he could not do anything about it. He knew she would find someone sooner or later after he left her. He could not prevent that, neither would he expect her to stay celibate the rest of her life. But this jealousy was killing him and preventing him from falling asleep. It had been more than three years since she had rejected his suggestion to come to the capital and five years since he'd left her in that beautiful Armenian meadow. He still couldn't stop thinking about her.

CHAPTER 33

Husrō-Parviz Seeks Advice

Farhad's love story disturbed Parviz. He knew human nature well and told himself. *There is this lovely maiden who is disappointed in the man she loved and then comes a handsome man who adores her and wants to give everything in exchange for her love. Will she pay attention to him? Or will she be loyal to me? The man who betrayed her and gave away her country and made her life far away from her people and her land.*

He felt guilty, but he did not want any man to get close to his only love. If he could not have her, he did not want anyone else to have her either. "Yes, it is selfish, I am selfish, but as long as she stays in love with me, someday we might be together. Will we? I doubt it, but there is a chance," he spoke aloud to the empty room.

He decided to ask his advisor and summoned his trusted prime minister, to come to his chamber for a private consultation. The King was deep in thought when the prime minister arrived. He saw his great King sitting majestically on his throne. His clothes were covered with jewelry. His belt and his hat were covered with rubies. But his face showed internal agony. He was wringing his hands in agitation.

He bowed. "Long live the King of Kings. I hope your years on the Persian Throne will be long and prosperous."

His salutation startled the King, but he motioned with his hand for the prime minister to sit down on the chair close to him. When he settled down, Bozorg-Mehr asked the King, "Your Majesty what is the problem and what can I do to help?"

"My dear advisor and teacher, I called you today to advise me of a personal problem I have. I do not want anyone to know about it."

"Of course, your Highness your secret is safe with me whether it is personal or public," Bozorg-Mehr answered calmly.

A faint smile appeared on the King's face when he started to reveal his disturbed feelings. "Dear Bozorg-Mehr you have been aware of my love for Princess Shirin since I was a Crown Prince and had no worries in the world. Unfortunately, life did not turn out the way we wanted. First, it was Bahram-Choobin who could have been the head of my army and would have won many wars for us, but he chose to fight against me and eventually lost his life. That fighting caused me to ask our enemies to help us. Although we achieved peace with the Romans, we had to give a big part of our country to them. And nobody knows the personal loss and sacrifice I had to endure to maintain this peace."

Bozorg-Mehr said, "My Lord, we know that you sacrificed your love for Princes Shirin to have peace and prosperity for your land and your people. Everyone knows and appreciates your sacrifice all over this vast land. However, I am puzzled by what has happened for you to now remember all these past problems? You are now the world's most powerful King and should not have any regrets or any worries."

A squeamish smile appeared on King's lips, and he said, "Oh, yes, I am the most powerful King, but that does not mean that

I don't regret my past actions. Have you ever been in love my friend?"

"Your honor, I thought your love was forgotten after having a lovely Queen and beautiful children. For most, the love for our offspring substitutes the love of our youth."

"I wish it was true. Yes, I love my children and was able to be content until now with my internal longing for the love of my youth. But now the burning sensation is back, and I cannot calm myself any longer."

"My Excellency, is this feeling caused by the news that another man is in love with Princess Shirin?"

"Yes, you guessed it right. I know he is innocent, and I cannot kill him, however, if I leave it the way it is, the burning sensation in my heart will kill me. I tried to forget, kept my days occupied with my country's affairs and my nights with wine and music, along with embracing the joys of playing with my children.

"But now, I feel I cannot think of anything but her. It seems that I am back to my youthful foolishness."

"Well, My Excellency you are still young, and apparently your heart is still enslaved to your feelings from five years ago. You are now the King of Kings. I hope you will be stronger than ever and hope you live as long as the world. I suggest you buy him with gold. We should ask him to come here and give him big hopes for his future. And then we shower him with gold like rays of sunshine. With gold people turn away from their religions. I am sure the gold will be sweeter than his love for Shirin. We have seen that people become blind with gold. You can make even an iron fist person lose his power with gold."

"What if you are wrong? You are an old man and do not remember the power of love in young hearts. Youth usually do not care about gold as much as the old do. From what I heard of this young man, I doubt that you will be able to dissuade him from his love."

"In that case, we need to give him a job that he cannot finish," Bozorg-Mehr replied.

The King liked this suggestion and asked him to find the engineer and bring him to his palace. So, the envoy found Farhad and asked him to accompany them to the capital. He did not know why the King had sent for him, but curiosity took over, and he decided to obey the order. He wanted to see and know his competition, so he went with the King's agents to the capital city. He was quiet all the way, thinking only of his love for Shirin.

When he got there, neither the luxury of the court nor the solemnity of the King affected him. By the King's order, he was seated on the top of the royal hall, very close to the curtain. The curtain was drawn, and the King's young face appeared. Everyone bowed before him.

When everyone was seated, at the point of a finger the King's agents showered Farhad with gold coins. Anyone else sitting in the palace would have been overjoyed since showering one with gold meant that he was very important, or he would become important in the court. But for Farhad, there was no difference between gold and dirt. When Parviz saw that Farhad did not even look at the gold coins pouring over his feet, he decided to talk to him.

He dismissed everyone but Farhad and the advisor that he'd spoken to before Farhad got to the court.

The King asked him, "Where are you from?"

"I am from the land of love."

"What are the occupations of people there? What kind of industry do they have?"

"They buy sadness and sell their souls."

King frowned and said, "It is not wise to sell your soul."

"It is not strange if you are in love."

"Did you fall in love with all your heart?"

"You are talking about the heart! I am speaking about my soul and my life."

"How much is your love for Shirin?"

"It is bigger than my precious life."

"Do you see her in your dreams like moonlight?"

"If I fall to sleep, but usually I cannot find rest."

"When will you clean your heart of her love?"

"When I am sleeping in my grave."

"If you were invited to her house what would you do?"

"I would throw my head to her feet."

"What if she plucks one of your eyes out?"

"I will give her my other eye."

"What if she never pays attention to you?"

"No problem. I can see her from afar as when I look at the moon."

"But it is not wise to just look at the moon from a distance."

"The farther the moon from turbulence, the better she is."

"What if she wants everything you have?"

"Oh, I am praying to my God that she does."

At this point, the King started to tell him his real intention and said, "Forget this love."

"I cannot forget her, do not ask this from a lover."

"This is a wild journey, relax and forget."

"Oh, relaxation is taboo for me."

"Go and be patient with this pain."

Farhad said, "You cannot ask my soul to be patient. The one who is not in love can be patient, but not the one who has a heart full of love."

"You are going to be destroyed by this love."

"What is better than being destroyed while being in love?"

"Do you know how many are in love with her?"

"Yes, but no one loves her as much as me."

"Are you scared of anything for her love?"

"Only the pain of separation from her."

"Forget her love and the assumption that she will be yours."

"How can I live without my sweet soul?"

"Do not talk about her; she is mine."

"Poor Farhad cannot do that."

"What if I look at her?"

"Everything around me will burn with my sadness."

The King whispered in Bozorg-Mehr's ear, "I am going to ask him for the impossible now."

Bozorg-Mehr shook his head in agreement, and Parviz told Farhad." Do you know why I asked that you come here?"

"No, to tell me to forget about my love?"

"That my friend is up to you since I know for sure you will not get anything but pain from it. However, I asked you to come here to do me a favor. We would like to construct a road, but there is a mountain in the way which makes road construction impossible. I want to cut down the mountain and make the road construction possible. I have not found anyone who could do it for me. I heard you are the only one who can do it. I need your help and will pay your wages in full. Can you do it for me?"

Farhad listened to the King. His expression changed from that of indifference to authority to a humble servant. He bowed his head and said, "I will serve my King and cut that mountain for you with the road you want. Will My Excellency then pay for my service with the kindness of your heart? Instead of wages, I want my King to promise me to forget about sweet Shirin as long as he lives."

Anger swept through Parviz like thunder. He wanted to kill the man right there and then. However, he told himself. *Why am I afraid of this promise? What he is going to attempt is on rock, not loose soil. This is an impossible job I am asking him to do, if he is not able to finish it, then my promise will not need to be tested.* So, with his warmest voice, he told Farhad, "I will guarantee your wish as a man, and the King of the Persian Empire, if you finish the road in less than ten months. Be assured that Kings never break their promises."

"Oh, My Excellency please let me know where this mountain is and where the road will be built."

"Between here and Zagros Mountain there is a road which we want to widen. This road is circles Bistoon Mountain, and we'd like it to cross the mountain instead. The road is important to us since it connects our capital cities, Tisfoon and Ecbatana."

"Your Majesty, I have heard and will obey. Your road will be built the way you want. I will leave now to attend to the project." Farhad bowed and left the court. He was jubilant. His rival was more interested in building the road than attending to his love. *Whatever everyone is saying is nonsense. She is lonely and unattached, and with enough love she will begin noticing me—and without any rival, she will be mine.* He started to travel toward the mountain with joy and happiness. It did not cross his mind that this was a plot to keep him away from Shirin.

CHAPTER 34

Farhad Starts His Project

Farhad arrived at Bistoon and began to work immediately. His first task was to carve in the mountainside Shirin's portrait. It was so beautiful that it looked like she was there looking at him. The curious people of the nearby village asked him what he was doing and who the portrait depicted. He explained his love for this beautiful Princess and his bet with the King.

A wise man from the crowd shook his finger at Farhad. "Do not play with fire. Only the portraits of the Kings have been carved into the stone for as long as we can remember. If the King hears about your carving, he will be mad enough to kill you."

"Oh the King is so kind, he told me if I finish this road he will forget about his sweetheart. However, I will carve his face also for his kindness and to prevent his anger." He carved Parviz and Shabdiz on the rock and then started to cut the mountain. As he worked, he sang his love songs to the mountain.

At the end of his workday, he sat before the portrait of his love and talked about his feeling. "Oh, why do I have so much granite to cut? I will not relax from cutting even if it costs my life." He sat there until the blackness of night overcame the day's light, talking to Shirin's picture.

"Oh, my idol, you are the cure for my injured heart; because of your love, my weak heart became foolish. I know that you do not think of me since you have better friends. While you still love Parviz, how can you remember me? Shirin is sitting happily with Parviz's love while poor Farhad is sacrificing his soul. It is your love, oh my candlelight, that makes me what you see. I am burning and I am patient from far away; I am like a butterfly who cannot tolerate the heat of the candle.

"I swear that if you kill me for my ardor, you will free me from this pain since death will be better than this life I have. For the sake of the first milk that your mother gave you, remember me. Even though you do not give me any sweet biscuits, my mouth becomes sweet with your name. I have no friend or companion except you. So, do not leave me. Please open your beautiful mouth and call me, so this night becomes day. Although I am poor, generously I will give my life for you. I had hope in my youthfulness. I had a lust for life. However, I am disappointed in both.

"I am the dust of your city. What wrong did you see from me? Tell me if, except for worshipping you, I have committed any crime? If I am the wind, and you are the free spirit looking toward me like the branch of the willow tree looks toward the wind. Oh, my dangerous treasure, if I am dirt you can make a temple from it. I wish you could hear my moaning just one night and see that I cannot sleep; even if your heart were made of stone, you would forgive this injured anguish of mine. You know I am like a straw, worthless of your love, but I break the mountain down with my bare hands. If the mountain cannot tolerate fighting with me, I am not afraid of any mountainous army who stands in front of me. If I wanted to fight Parviz, I would win against Shabdiz, his stallion, in the fight. What am I to do?"

He worked long hours and kept singing his love songs as he continued working and talking. "Oh, my sweet fairy have you notice that Parviz, Shirin, and Farhad all have six letters in our names? Then if all of our names are made of six letters, isn't it strange that his six wins? Oh the world's brightest candle, for your love, I am relaxed neither day nor night. The person who gave me this job demanded my life. This job is so hard that dying is easy in comparison.

"Although I do not have gold or silver to throw at your feet, my yellowish skin, and my tears could be your gold and silver. I am alone in this world; I do not have any friend to help me up if I fall. If I sit in a well for hundred years, I will not see anyone at the top of the well; I will only hear my sigh. If I run into the desert and mountains, I will not see anyone following me but my own shadow."

Every night he cried until he fell asleep, and every morning he began again to cut the stone. The road nearby was crowded, and some decided to visit the crazy lover who sang and talked to himself. They heard him and were amused by the work he had done. Most often, they gathered around the carvings on the top of the mountain and admired Shirin's beauty or the artful carving of their King and his famous horse. The story of his love was told and retold and spread across the world. This caused others to visit him, and they were astonished to see such a beautiful carving of the two faces.

CHAPTER 35

⊶———⊷

Shirin Visits Farhad on the Mountain

One day Shirin was sitting with her friends, and they were talking. Some spoke of the past and their beautiful homeland. Homayoon suggested, "Let's talk about future happiness since dwelling on memories can make us sad. I am sure we will have lots of fun in the future."

Shirin shook her head in agreement and said, "Yes, of course, we will have a good time here my friend. Every day has its beauty, and we can find happiness within our souls, not from the places we live. I would like to know what the news is. Anything interesting?"

Farangis winked and said, "The only news we hear these days is all the talk about Farhad's love for you."

Shirin said thoughtfully. "I was wondering this morning why he does not visit us anymore? It has been a couple of months now."

Golnoosh said, "That is because he is carving your face on the rock of Bistoon Mountain and spends his day looking at it, and talking to it, or crying at its feet."

Shirin frowned. "Why is he doing this? Where? Bistoon Mountain?"

Farangis said, "He is making the road that our King ordered him to build in order to have you."

Shirin, who was a little bit disturbed when she heard the King named, shifted in her seat. "I do not understand! Can one of you please tell me everything you have heard?"

Homayoon said, "If you give me the honor, I will."

"Of course, tell me everything from the beginning."

"Well Your Majesty, apparently the news of building your castle and waterway to get fresh milk every day reached our Lord, the King of Kings. He summoned Farhad and asked him to make a road for him, cutting through Bistoon Mountain. Parviz promised that when Farhad finished the road, he would give you to him. That is why Farhad is so determined to build this road through the middle of the mountain."

Shirin grew furious and cried out, "What are you talking about? I am not property! The King cannot give me to anyone. Besides, why should he do such a thing? The road around that mountain is excellent. He does not need any road to be built there!"

Farangis interrupted her and said, "Forgive me, My Lady. Don't you see? Our King knows how hard it is to build a road there. He did that to keep Farhad from seeing you."

She frowned. "So, the engineer is so stupid that he did not notice it?"

Homayoon said, "Nobody knows what happened when Farhad visited the King. But according to the story that Fahad told visitors, the King gave him gold, and he refused. Then he threatened him and said he should forget your Highness, which he rejected entirely without any fear. The King then asked him to build the road and promised to pay him what he asked. Farhad said that he wanted the King to forget his love for Shirin if Farhad finished the road. To Farhad's surprise, our King accepted the challenge. And promised that if he completed the road in ten months, he would do just that." He paused a little and said, "As Farangis mentioned, our King does not think he can finish the job. His Majesty just does not want him close to our lady."

A fist of emotion hit Shirin. The thought of her lover always made her heart beat faster and the blood rise to her face. However, anger and surprise were now added to her earlier feelings. *So, he can have fun with his new Queen, but I should not have a lover around me! I see that Shah-Pour is always missing from my court since he gets summoned by the King so often. Is he that jealous?* The thought crossed her mind and made her laugh aloud.

Her companions did not say anything. They did not know why she was laughing, but they were happy that the news did not affect her severely. They waited for her long, fascinating laugh to end.

Finally, she said, "Well, well. In this case, I will go to Mount Bistoon today. I want to see how Farhad's iron arms cut the rock. Who knows, maybe from that iron and stone someday I will get a single spark."

She asked to saddle her horse. She remembered that she had let Shah-Pour ride Golgoon to Tisfoon so he could get back faster. So, she requested to saddle another horse. She left looking as beautiful as early spring flowers. As slim as she was, she was riding the horse like a bird. She got close to the mountain and rode her horse up the rough rocks. Farhad was cutting the stones and, as usual, talking and singing love songs when he saw her horse coming up the mountain.

As soon Shirin got close, he dropped his ax and bent down in front of her and said, "Oh my moon you heard my cry and lightened my darkness with your visit."

"Hello Farhad, everyone is talking about your art, and I've come to see and admire it."

"Oh, My Lady, I am naught but the dust of your city. Please

come down and see if I was able to show one-thousandth of your beauty in my carving."

Shirin dismounted her horse and handed a jug of milk to him. "Take this and drink it for me."

"Oh, my angel you knew how thirsty I was to see you." Then he drank from it.

Shirin looked at the carvings and was amused by their accuracy. "I heard that your sculptures of my face and the King were accurate, and I believe it as I look at them now."

"Oh, Queen of beauty, nobody can carve your face as beautiful as you are. Not even me. The portrait is only slightly like you."

Shirin laughed and said, "You always exaggerate when you talk about me. It is getting late, and I must go back."

Farhad bowed and said, "Thank you so much for visiting me. You brightened my day and my night. You gave me hope. I hope you will visit me again."

Shirin smiled and said, "It was a pleasure seeing your marvelous work. The door to my castle is always open to you." Then she mounted the horse and started down the mountain.

However, the horse was so scared of the height that it would not walk more than a few steps. Shirin kept whipping the horse. It moved a few steps but then halted completely when finally, its heart stopped. Shirin almost fell but Farhad was there and took the horse and its rider on his shoulder and carried them down the mountain. He put Shirin down when he reached the bottom. Shirin was amused by his action and thanked him for saving her life.

"My Lady you are my soul and I worship you. What I did was my pleasure." He bowed and went back to the top of the mountain to cut the rocks. His heart was warm with love and hope. *She has noticed me. I was right in accepting this hard job. She came to see me and who knows what the future holds?* He started cutting with more force and determination. The work grew easier, and it felt like the rock was as soft as dirt.

Shirin and her companions went back to her castle. Farhad was too happy to imagine. He was working faster. The job seemed easier. The progress was incredible. Parviz's agents who were observing the advancement of the job decided to report the incident.

CHAPTER 36

Husrō-Parviz Hears About Shirin's Visit to Bistoon

The heads of the armed forces, the ministers, the heads of state, and the foreign consular all were waiting in the majestic hall of the palace. The walls of the lobby featured a beautiful painting of Shah Anoshiravan, the father of Shah Hormozd, on a hunting trip with other Kings. Those in the hall were amused by the dazzling luxury of the place.

Silk curtains opened, and the young King's face appeared. He was sitting on his golden throne wearing a silk tunic, which was covered with gems, and a pink vest with many pearls sewed on its edge. He had on pleated pants which were fastened to his ankles by a thin thread. The most magnificent of the scene was his crown, with dazzling rubies, emeralds, and pearls. He was a tall, handsome man with curly hair spread to his shoulders and a long beard. His belt was fastened tightly around his waist to show his perfect build.

The Mobed started his prayer, "In the name of Ahura Mazda, I pray for His Majesty's well-being and for His Majesty to add more lands to his Empire."

Then each, in turn, reported their findings to the King. The foreign consulares gave the King reports and offered their gifts. When all were finished, the King said, "You now have my permission to withdraw." Soon the gathering was done, and everyone except his advisor left the hall.

Bozorg-Mehr bowed and said, "Great King who will be healthy and sturdy, our observer from Bistoon has arrived. I have not had a chance to talk to him. Should he come in and give his report?"

The King's heart raced. He knew that his prime minister had agents all over the country to report anything unusual to him. He had asked his prime minister to send a few spies where Shirin had her castle to watch her movements. He said in a calm voice that hid his internal discomfort, "Yes, my friend, please ask him to come in."

A dusty young man arrived and after the usual salutation, told the King of Shirin's visit and Farhad's action that saved her life.

The King thanked the soldier, and the man took his leave. When there was no one but the King and his minister, Parviz asked, "What do you think of this news?"

"My Lord, I heard from another agent that since this incident Farhad is excelling in his work. There is an estimate that if he continues working this way, the road will be finished soon."

"So instead of pushing him away from her, I made her closer to him. She visited him, and now he is happy and hopeful. What stupid advice you gave me."

Bozorg-Mehr was frightened now since he realized that his advice added to the King's worries. He said, "Well I was wrong about the estimation of his power. I never thought he could do such hard work. I advised you with that assumption. However, I know a way to end this problem."

"What are you going to do?"

"Well, if Farhad gets disappointed by Shirin, he will stop

working. That will give you a chance to fire him. I will find some-one who can give him bad news, and we will see."

"What if he does not believe your man?"

"My Lord, let me worry about that."

"All right, but please be careful, I do not want this to backfire like your last advice."

"I will My Lord."

Bozorg-Mehr found a man who was willing to do any das-tardly thing. He gave him money and told him to go and tell Farhad that Shirin had suddenly passed away. The man accepted the assignment and went to Bistoon Mountain. He saw a man with arms made of steel. He looked like a wild runaway from captivity, a lion, or a drunken elephant cutting the mountain. Farhad's heart was warm from Shirin's love and because of the flame of love inside, he was unaware of himself or the world. He was singing in memory of Shirin's beautiful face. Like hot iron, he was hitting his ax on the rocks. The cold-hearted man went toward Farhad, loosed his tongue and said, "Oh hello there. What are you doing here? Are you stupid to work so hard?"

"I am doing this job for the joy which comes from the name of my love. Oh, she is a friend who is a sweet talker, and she is sweeter to me than my own life."

The sour-faced man opened his bitter tongue with a big sigh and said, "Oh my, Shirin has died. Are you not aware of it?"

"No. No that is not true, how can it be? Why?"

"Did you not hear that the wind of death dropped that beau-tiful cypress tree to the ground? They have already buried her. They cried so much, and there was a big funeral, it was a sudden illness—nobody knew from where it came. It is such a pity that such a beautiful maiden lost her life."

Farhad at first just looked at the stranger and listened to his disturbing speech. Then he cried out. "Oh, I am in pain, and before any cure comes, I will die of the anguish. That beautiful cyprus is under the soil? I have to pour dirt on my head. The petals of this flowering shrub are gone, so the orchard is now a prison to me. The world's candlelight is gone, so how come my day has not turned to night? I am cold because the light is dead. The sun is yellow since my moon is gone. Oh, I will reach Shirin in the other world so I will run to death." At that moment, he threw his ax down and jumped and plummeted from the mountain like a ton of rock. He was still calling Shirin's name when he reached the bottom and died.

The deceitful man stood with wide eyes. Several other curious people who had climbed up the mountain saw that Farhad had jumped down. They had come to observe his work and hear his songs and admire his carving, but they were instead witness to his crazy act of suicide, and they didn't know why. The sadness sat in their hearts and the news spread.

There grew a legend that day that the engineer's ax was made from a live pomegranate branch; that he always acquired a fresh branch so it would stay soft in his hands. When he heard the stranger's story, Farhad threw his ax and the blade went into the rock. Its arm, though, planted in the soft dirt of Mount Bistoon. From it grew a pomegranate tree which bore many pomegranates every year. It became famous since it was said that the fruit of that tree would cure the illness of any who ate from it.

CHAPTER 37

The Bad News Reaches Shirin

Shah-Pour reached Shirin's Castle, unsaddled his horse and fed him. Then he left the stable and was about to enter the castle to change his clothing when he saw a tall rider coming toward him. He recognized Farshid and frowned. He and Farshid were traveling together from Tisfoon. However, Farshid told him that he was going to visit Mount Bistoon to see the carving, then he planned to go to Ecbatana. So, at the fork, they had departed in different directions. *What is he doing here? Maybe he decided to travel here to rest before his journey.* Farshid stopped in front of him and dismounted his horse. His face was white, and he looked disturbed.

Shah-Pour said with a cheerful voice. "Hello, Farshid what a joy to see you again. Welcome. Did you visit the engineer?"

Farshid replied "Hello my friend. Thank you for your hospitality. Yes, I went there, and I wish I did not go. I wish I did not see that awful event."

"What are you talking about? Which event?"

Farshid, who had tears in his eyes, said, "You told me Farhad was your friend from the time you were going to school, so I thought you should hear the news. I heard that he has no family close by."

Shah-Pour, who was now worried, grabbed Farshid's shoulder and asked, "Who are you talking about? What happened that has disturbed you so?"

"I am talking about Farhad, my friend. I have witnessed his death, and I am sorry to tell you the bad news."

Shah-Pour's hand dropped, and he asked with much sorrow, "Did you say Farhad died. How? When?"

"I and several others were climbing Mount Bistoon and were almost at the top when we saw it. A man was talking to Farhad when he threw his ax and jumped off the cliff. We ran down and saw him dead on the ground. People there told me he was calling to Shirin when he hit the ground."

Tears gathered in Shah-Pour's eyes, and he asked, "Did you talk to the man speaking to him? Does he know what caused him to jump?"

"We did, but he said the engineer wasn't making any sense. Farhad told him if he dies he will meet Shirin in the other world. Apparently, he gave up hope and decided to commit suicide."

Shah-Pour shook his head side to side and said, "Knowing Farhad I do not think he was giving up. He had to hear something awful to kill himself." Then he said, "I have to let her Royal Majesty hear the news. Can you please come with me and let her know? I do not have the stomach to give her this awful news."

Shirin was sitting in her luxurious hall as beautiful as ever. Her friends and servants were sitting around passing the wine and were chatting when Shah-Pour asked permission to enter.

Shirin with her sweet smile pointed to the dusty men. "Come in my friend. What brought you here so dusty? It seems that you just arrived and did not have time to change."

Shah-Pour bowed and said, "My Royal Highness, you are right.

140

My friend Farshid here has disturbing news that your Highness needs to know. Please give him your permission."

Shirin's heart dropped. As any person in love, her worries were about the King. She wanted to ask if something had happened to Parviz, but she controlled her emotions and said, "You have my permission. Tell me the news."

Farshid bowed and said in a sad voice. "Your Majesty, this morning Farhad jumped off the mountain Bistoon and died. It is stated that he has no relatives, but Your Majesty had a kind heart toward him. So, I thought to let you know as soon as possible."

Color evaporated from Shirin's face. Tears appeared in her beautiful eyes. "Jumped off the mountain? Are you sure? Is it possible that he fell off the cliff?"

"Your Majesty it seemed that he jumped to my eyes, but anything is possible."

Shah-Pour said, "My Royal Highness, apparently a man was standing by his side talking to him. But according to the witnesses, he did not touch him before he leapt down." Shirin asked, "Did anyone ask him what his business was there and what happened, why he jumped?"

Farshid bowed and said, "My Lady, we did. He said he was just another person observing the work. But Farhad was disturbed when he saw the man. The man claimed Farhad told him, "If I die I will meet Shirin in the other world.""

A surge of sadness overcame her. *He died for me! He wanted to join me in heaven!* She spoke in a very calm voice that covered her sorrow. "With my permission, everyone withdraw so I can speak to Shah-Pour."

The audience bowed one by one and left the hall. Shirin sat down and let tears pour from her beautiful eyes. Shah-Pour's eyes misted with his own depression. The silence covered the room while they both mourned their dear friend. Then Shirin spoke.

"My dear Shah-Pour, I cannot believe that a young and healthy man like Farhad is gone."

"Your Highness I know, it is hard for me to believe it, but it is a fact of life. When it is time for a person to go the misfortune will arise from somewhere. If he grasps a branch full of blooms, instead of flowers, stones will hit his head. He will be so sad that he cannot find any way out other than just to give up and die. Any minute particle that the wind brings, it could be the dust of mighty Kings. Who knows how old this world is and how it was hundred years ago? Every century there are different people and events, but the people from the previous century will not see these changes. It is magnificent to be in love and die happy with that love."

Shirin sighed and said in a low voice, "That is the most disturbing thing in my mind. Do you think I was the cause of his death? Did he die for me?"

"Your Highness he worshiped you. You could not cause his death. He was so happy just to see you from a distance, and you did not give him anything but generosity and respect."

Shirin frowned and said, "His last word was that if he dies, he will be meeting me in the other world. What do you make of this statement? Why should he want to die to join me? Did he think I had died?"

Shah-Pour said with admiration, "My Lady you are very smart; the thought crossed my mind too, but I could not find any reason why he would think that."

"Is it possible that the stranger who was talking to him told him I died, and that is why he jumped off the cliff?"

"My Lady anything is possible, but what would motivate that man to speak such a lie?"

A sad smile appeared on Shirin's face. "He did not have any motivation, but his employer did I bet."

Shah-Pour asked curiously. "His employer? Your Highness! Who are you talking about?"

"I am talking about our beloved King, of course."

"Oh, My Lady you are not telling me the man had orders from our beloved King to deliver such a cruel deception?"

"I heard of Farhad's assignment by our King. The task did not make sense especially since it was said that the agreement between them was about me. I was told that the assignment was a deliberate act to take Farhad away from me. I was mad. I do not believe I belong to the King and did not think he could give me away, so I decided to tease him and went to see Farhad."

She paused and then said, "That is why I am so disturbed. I think that my visit was the reason for Farhad's accident."

Shah-Pour, who was looking at her with wonder, said, "Your Excellency how can you assume such a cruel behavior like this from our beloved King?"

"My friend, we love him and as people say love is blind. But if you forget your love you would say, he is a mighty King, and he can do anything he fancies. Have you not heard that power corrupts people?"

"We both know him My Lady, and yes we love him for his kindness and his good nature. I cannot believe that he did such a nonsensical thing."

"Oh, what does not make sense my friend? Can you explain?"

"Of course, your Highness knows that a King can order his soldiers to shoot whoever he likes. Farhad was disturbed long before his suicide. He was running all over places and lived with animals all day and would come at night to drink milk in your pool. If our King wanted him gone, he would have been gone long ago. He could have ordered someone to kill him and bury him without a trace. We would think that he left the area. It was after Farhad met the King that he started working again. It seemed that

143

making the road made him sane after months of madness. Now let's say someone told Farhad that, God forbid, Your Highness died. Any reasonable person would try to see if there is any truth in the news, anyone in their right mind would investigate. He should have wanted to see you for the last time instead of jumping off that cliff. I assume that it was his sickness and not any person that killed him."

"Well I hope you are right, I never had any attraction to him. He was handsome and sincere and convincing. I loved his love song and the love he bestowed on me. So many times I wished I could love him back, or had any attraction to him. Nevertheless, I miss him as a dear friend. I heard that his body is still lying down there, and he has no relatives. I want to arrange the best funeral that you can arrange for him and make a dome over his grave."

"My Lady be assured that I will see to your order right away."

The funeral was magnificent. Princess Shirin was there with tearful eyes. All the Princess's companions and servants and people who admired the late engineer's work and songs also attended the funeral. They talked about what a pity it was to lose such a young and handsome artist.

After the funeral, Shah-Pour asked Princess Shirin if he could take the news to the King. She agreed and asked him to see if he could find any hint that the King had anything to do with it. He promised and told her he was sure he would not find anything.

CHAPTER 38

⸻⸺○⸺⸻

Husrō-Parviz's Sympathy Letter to Shirin

The cold-hearted man came back and brought the news to Bozorg-Mehr. It was late in the evening, and the King was about to retire when Bozorg-Mehr asked permission to enter.

"Come in my friend."

"The prime minister bowed and said, "Long live the King of Kings, the Lord of the Persian Empire, the light of seven countries."

"The light of Ahura Mazda upon you. What brings you here this afternoon? Any problems with our land?"

"By the grace of God, everything is calm throughout the Persian Empire, and there are no worries for Your Highness."

Husrō-Parviz looked at the old man and inquired with his eyes. "I heard that there is an important issue you wanted to discuss."

"Yes, Your Highness. I wanted to tell you the thorn you were concerned about is gone."

"What are you talking about?"

"The engineer died two days ago."

The news startled him, so he asked with concern, "What happened and how? He was so young and healthy!"

"He killed himself after he got the news that the Princess was dead."

Husrō-Parviz narrowed his eyes and asked, "Did your agent tell him that the Princess Shirin was dead?"

"Yes, Your Majesty. I thought the news would stop him from the job, and you would be able to break your agreement."

"But he killed himself, and his blood is on our hands."

"No, My Lord, he committed suicide."

"Yes, could we not have given him different news like the Princess was falling in love with somebody?"

"My Lord that would not have stopped him. He knew that the Princess was in love with you, and he told you that it was okay. He was happy to see her from a distance. In fact, he was worshipping her picture that was carved in the rock. I did not think he would kill himself, though. I thought he would stop working and would go to see if the news was true. Then we would tell him the bet was off since he stopped working."

"Thank you for the information. I am tired, and with my permission, you can leave now."

The old man bowed and left the King to drown in his thoughts. *I wish I had never said anything to anyone. His advice was terrible one after another. That young man had not done any wrong except fall in love. He did not deserve to die.*

He remembered the tall, handsome soul who left his court smiling to do the job he was ordered to do.

This sadness had occupied the King for several days when Shah-Pour arrived and asked to see him. With obvious joy, he said, "Let him in please."

Shah-Pour came in, bowed and said, "Long live the King of Kings, the light of seven countries."

Husrō-Parviz looked at his friend and said, "Hello Shah-Pour, come and sit by me. I need your company more than ever."

Shah-Pour sat in the chair next to the King and said, "It is my honor, My Lord, that you like my company."

"Tell me, my friend, how is my love?"

"My Lord, these days she is mourning the loss of a friend. Farhad has left her, and she is sorrowful."

Jealousy crept inside Parviz's heart, but he tried to ignore it and said, "Oh, I did not know that they were that close."

Shah-Pour asked surprisingly, "Did not Your Majesty know about Farhad's love for Shirin?"

"Oh yes, he did not hide it from anyone that he was madly in love with her, but I did not know that she had any feeling for him."

"Oh, My Lord he was her friend, and she is mourning the loss of a friend, not a lover sir."

"I understand, I saw him only once but I was sad to hear the news. It is a pity that such a young, handsome and brave man fell to mental illness. While I cannot do anything about it, I am worried about my love."

"My Lord, our Princess is a lonely young woman with a lover that she cannot be with. She occupies herself with hunting, riding and spending time with her companions. But we both know it is not enough for a beautiful lady like the Princess. Farhad was an assurance for her that she still is attractive and loveable. Now she is back to the dark corner of bitterness and loneliness. Yes, she mourns his death since she knows how Farhad felt, and she misses his devotion and the feeling that someone loved her so deeply. She made a tomb for him, and she visits it every day and cries. I know that she never had any romantic feelings for him, but still, she cries."

Each word of Shah-Pour was a dagger in his heart and made him sad. He sighed and said, "I wish I could hold her in my arms and tell her that she always will be attractive to me. I want to tell her I am still madly in love with her."

Shah-Pour bent his head and said, "I am sure these are her wishes too. Unfortunately, your destiny is different than hers, and you two have to take separate roads."

"I know the reality. I'd like to send her a letter of condolence. Will you take it to her?"

"Oh, My Lord, your orders are always my commands."

"Go and rest tonight, I will give you the letter tomorrow. I can trust only you to take back and forth my messages to her."

"I know Your Royal Majesty, and your confidence honors me."

Husrō-Parviz wrote: *To the Queen of beauty my forever love, the sweet Shirin whom the lovers of sugar call Shakar Khand (sweet smile or laugh) since your smile is much sweeter than sugar. I heard you are mourning the death of a friend and pouring warm tears from those narcissus eyes. Your cyprus-like stature is bent down out of sadness. You are crying in the memory of a friend so fiercely that the whole world is burning down. That is the proper way to treat a friend, and that's the way of friendship my darling. God pardoned that porter who was cutting and climbing the mountain to its knees. The stranger who was crying so loud with his beautiful poems of love died so young. The world should be asked to cry for him. A lover who dies of sadness like him, compels us to learn a lesson. His sudden death shook me and has also made me sad. I am so worried about you though. I know that you are so worried for him, that although he is dead, you are not leaving him. I am wondering why you killed him with your beauty and ignorance?*

He died from the pain of loving you. I know that if you sit on his soil for hundreds of years, you will not find a humbler or better worshiper of Shirin than he. But crying will not benefit anyone. I know that you have done enough mourning, but you cannot fight destiny. Everybody's life always ends with death, and nobody will live forever. You are the day, and he was a bright star in the sky. When the day appears the star dies, you know. You are the morning, and he was a light in the night, and the light has to die when the morning appears. You are like a candle, and he was like a drunken butterfly who died for his candle. You are fire, and he was the aloes-wood who would burn when the fire appears. However, if a bird has flown out of your orchard, the eagle still worships your sky. If a drop of water falls out of your pitcher, there are so many rivers still coming your way. If Farhad died, I hope Shirin will live. There is no pity if a yellow flower dies. I want my beautiful jonquil to live forever.

I love you forever darling,
Husrō-Parviz

The next morning Shah-Pour took the King's letter to Princess Shirin. Shirin had just come back from her hunting trip when she learned that Shah-Pour was waiting for her. As she arrived, he rose and greeted her. Then he took the letter and said, "His Royal Majesty gave me this letter to give you." He bowed to Shirin and offered the letter in his hand.

A surge of joy went through Shirin's body. She took the letter and kissed it three times and then broke the seal and started to read it. She read the letter and reread it.

The words began to dance in front of her. She saw them as sugar cane with a snake around them. She told Shah-Pour, "I do not know why I love this man so much. He talks about loving me but at the same time blaming me for Farhad's death! He challenged him, and when he was almost done with the challenge he ordered his sentence and now he blames my love for it."

Shah-Pour, who was surprised to see her anger after seeing her joy, said, "Forgive me My Lady but I do not think what happened to Farhad is anyone's fault. It came from his own internal turmoil. Our King is very much in love with you and though he cannot steal glance of your face, but he continues to live and rule an Empire as large as Persia. Your Highness is also in love with our King, but you are not killing yourself. However, Farhad committed suicide. I loved him and admired his ability, however, I cannot blame anyone for his loss of life but himself. I assure you that our King did not have anything to do with his death. His Majesty was sorrowful when I saw him, and I heard from several others that he was sorry for the accident."

"If that is true, why did he blame me for it?"

"My Lady, I do not know what he said in his letter. But when I told him about your mourning for the loss of our friend I sensed jealousy at the same time as sadness for not being with you now. He loves you dearly My Lady."

CHAPTER 39

Queen Maryam Dies

Destiny plays tricks that nobody can predict. In 601, Princess Maryam grew sick and died, and in the same year, Caesar Maurice was murdered by his General Phocas, who usurped the Roman throne. Both events freed Parviz from obligations. He owed his throne to the Roman Empire but the Empire was dead, and he was free.

His ten years of marriage had brought peace to the whole country. His wife gave him seven sons and two daughters. He respected her and felt he owed his throne to her and her father. Although their marriage was not based on love, he still appreciated her status.

When Princess Maryam died, he was free to grow like the maryam plant. However, he still wanted to keep face. She was a political wife, and the politics had to be played out even in her death. He held a dignified funeral for her. He did not sit on his throne for a month, and he wore black as a sign of mourning.

When Shirin heard of Maryam's death, she felt both a bud and a thorn in her heart. She became happy since she was going to be free of jealousy, but also was sad since she was wise and knew that it could happen to her. For the sake of Parviz, she stopped showing her happiness and did not do anything.

After several months had passed, she heard that Parviz was back on his throne. Her heart asked her to sow the seed of lust and write Parviz a letter like the one she had received after Farhad's death. The words she had in her heart were planted in the message like planting seeds in dirt.

> *To the King of Kings who forgives even repenting crim-inals. The King who feeds people and without any pen writes on the stone like a ruby. In His Majesty's land, nobody is sad even in the sea or on the mountain. You are the sunshine of the sky who is commander of seven countries. In this time His Majesty has everything from the moon to fishes in the sea, and he knows everything from the sky to the earth.*
>
> *His Majesty knows that day and night have two dif-ferent colors and life sometimes is like sugar and other times like poison. In this world, we see both funerals and weddings. Although the King's bride is under the dirt, there is no worry; the King will have other brides. Destiny took her early because it knew the King and the fact that he would soon grow tired of her. She was the best companion for you, however, do not worry my King; there are many others. Soon you will be looking at another rose garden and will pick another bud.*
>
> *Oh, my tender-hearted King, do not suffer since she was a treasure who should be under dirt anyway. Do not worry since worries will not add to your life. It is better if you forget Maryam since even if you were to*

become Jesus, you would not find her. Drink wine. Why are you pouring your tears when you know that everyone who is born will die someday? You should accept her death. Do not burden the dead with mourning since they want our patience, not cries. You should know that when it is time to die there is no difference between beggars and Kings.

If a cyprus tree is dried out, you who are the world's soul should live. You are like a pearl and ruby which look better alone. Do not worry if that gem is gone. You are like a mine and never will be without gems. If one deer runs away from your land, let it be since there are so many like her. If an idol is lost, don't worry, Kasra is alive. If Jesus is alive, do not worry about Maryam.

With all my love,
Your noble friend, Shirin

CHAPTER 40

Husrō-Parviz Without Maryam

Since his own General Phocas murdered Ceasar Maurice, Parviz had a reason to cancel his agreement with the Romans and take back Persia's lost lands. He prepared for war against Phocas. Parviz finished his meeting with his advisors about the new war, then permitted for everyone to leave.

Just then, Shah-Pour asked permission to enter. He gave Shirin's letter to the King. Parviz was so happy to see his lover's letter he opened it with joy and started to read. When he finished it, he laughed and said, "Oh this is the answer to my letter, not a message to start a war between us, not now. Tell her I am madly in love with her and I wish to see her as soon as possible. We are going to war in less than twenty days, and I would like to see her beautiful face as quickly as possible."

Then he sent for jewelry worth a fortune to be brought in, thinking he would see her before the war.

Shah-Pour took the jewelry and said, "Long live the King of Kings. I will tell her your demand. I will either bring her or her answer back here."

"Thank you, Shah-Pour, now I am tired and need to go to bed. Good night."

Shah-Pour bowed and said, "Good evening to the great King of my heart."

CHAPTER 41

Shirin's Answer to the King's Demand

Shah-Pour gave the jewelry and message to Shirin. Shirin frowned and said, "After all these times giving me Hell, now he is ordering me to go to him! No, he is our King, but I still want him to treat me like a Queen, not a slave."

"But my Royal Highness, he is in love with you and wants to be with you. I am sure he will marry you and make you his Queen as soon as you go to him."

"Well he did not call on me all these times, and I cannot forget his past actions. However, I would like to answer him myself. I am going to write him, and you can take the letter to him."

"I will obey as you wish My Lady."

She wrote:

Oh King of Kings, you own the world and your flag is all over this land. From China to Rome your signature is known. Any cookies that we eat we eat for its sweet taste, however, I am that cookie except my sweet name does not have any sugar in it. Yes, as soon as I came to this world I was in love with you and wanted you with my heart and soul. I never looked for anybody nor worshiped anyone but you. However, I did not see any kindness from you. What you call love is only lust since you do not know the meaning of love. You are the King, and the world is praising you. I want someone to worship me. Please let me stay in my loneliness and be happy with the many women who are surrounding you.

Love, Shirin

When Parviz got the letter, he became angry. His heart told him he needed to see Shirin right away, but his wisdom advised him to forget her. His heart said I will not forget that beautiful love of mine even if I get hit by many stones. His wisdom said this is nonsense, be patient and stop disgracing yourself. *You are not a baby to be deceived by cookies. If you do not want to fall, you climb a ladder step by step. You claim that you captured a lion, but a deer stands up bravely to you?*

He could not tell anyone how he felt. He was in love, but he also was a proud King whose orders were obeyed by everyone, except his lost lover. She was telling him she loved him but refused to come close. The thought came to his mind. He knew that Shah-Pour was Shirin's dear friend, and he was the one whom Shirin confided in. So, he decided to keep him in his court in hopes that Shirin would get lonely and stop her stubbornness.

He looked at Shah-Pour, who was sitting motionless in front of him waiting to hear his thoughts. The King said, "I am going to the war with the Romans, and I want you to be with me as my eyes and ears till I come back. After I come back, I'd like you to stay with me as my closest and dearest friend and advisor."

Shah-Pour was so surprised at such an offer that he could not say anything for a moment. Then he overcame his shock and said, "Oh my Royal Highness your kindness is beyond my ability to thank you. It will be my pleasure to be so close to My Lord and I hope I am worthy of the honor you have given me."

Husrō-Parviz smiled and said, "You accept it then!"

"Of course, Your Majesty, who can refuse such an honor? When do you want me to start?"

"Right away, of course, we are leaving by the end of the week, and I want you to get acquainted with your new job."

"But my Highness, Princess Shirin is expecting me to go back. I need to talk to her about my new assignment."

"Yes, I know she is expecting you. But you can send someone to tell her about your new job, of course. If you want the job."

"Oh, your Highness knows how much I love you and how happy to be close to My Lord."

"That is set then. Go and rest. I will ask my advisor to start training you for the job early tomorrow morning. With my permission, you can retire now."

Shah-Pour bowed and left the King.

CHAPTER 42

Shirin's Loneliness and Sadness

Shirin was waiting for Parviz's letter, but her expectation brought no fruits. Days went by with no news from her lover. Worse was the fact that Shah-Pour also vanished from her life. She received a message from him that he was accompanying Shah-Hanshah in his quest toward Rome.

Every day she occupied herself with hunting and riding and talking with her companions, however when the sky hugged the night, and the sun forgot the lands of the east she became disturbed. She had a hard time sleeping when there was no Mobed to read Zand for her. Neither were there any singing birds. Shirin's heart was stunned and dark as the night itself. She wondered, *Oh, is this night or a constant nuisance? This is not night; it is a black snake or wild eaten animal. Oh, what happened to the blue sphere that this night is not like the other nights? Maybe the smoke of my heart has stopped you, or tears have stung your feet? I cannot bear this sadness nor do I see any sign of the dawn. I am that candle that is burning all night, and like a candle, I am crying every night. Oh, birds, sing if you have any tongues. Oh God, change my night to a day and make me successful in the world.*

My hope is gone and my nights are so black from lack of hope. My sadness would kill even the strongest man. Please make me happy so that I can fight this depression. Oh God, you who help anyone who asks your advice, please lend me a hand. I urge you over the tears of children. Please help me to get rid of this sadness. If each hair of mine becomes a tongue, each one of them will be talking about your greatness. You are the God of beginning and the end that no one comprehends. We cannot do anything but surrender. It is you who make one wealthy or take him to die. Please do what you think is right. I am sure it is your power which made me so strong. However, please, I cannot tolerate this pain anymore.

So, this way she passed her time. She was waiting without knowing what she was waiting for. Her days and nights dragged slowly.

CHAPTER 43

Parviz Goes to Shirin's Palace

Ḵusrō-Parviz, along with Shahrbaraz and his other best generals, quickly captured Dara and Edessa. They recaptured lost territory in the north, which made the Sasanian-Byzantine borders return to the pre-591 boundaries before Parviz gave Maurice territory in return for military aid. After having reclaimed the lost territory, Parviz withdrew from the battlefield and handed military operations over to Shahrbaraz and Shahin Vahmanzadegan. He was back home proud and happy for his victories. His long wish was fulfilled, and he did not feel sorry for losing part of his homeland, but when he was not at war, his heart demanded its request. He wanted to be with the woman he loved and did not see anything preventing him from being with her except his pride.

Two years after his wife's death, in the early morning, he decided to go hunting. The roaring of drums and the cry of the windpipe rose. The flags went up, and the men mounted their horses. The greatest King came out with all the other crowned lords, such as Faghfour and Fysoor, surrounding him. As a piece of cloud covers the moon, his banner flew over the King's head.

His golden swords were fastened to his waist like a golden fence

161

so no one could get too close to him. The clamor of drums on the backs of elephants covered the desert for miles. Hundreds of water carriers washed his steps. Hundreds of censer holders poured sweet incense into the fire. If a stranger were crossing that road, he would know it was the King who was passing by.

That was the way he left town. But his army did not have any idea where he was going when he told them he was going to take a hunting trip. He rode his horse like a flying bird. He went from one hunt to another in the desert and mountains for a week. Even the eagles could not hide from him.

However, he did not stay in one place until he got close to Shirin's palace. When it was about 30 kilometers to her home, he dismounted his horse. It was winter, and cold weather was creeping in. The King ordered the set up of tents and the start of fires.

Once the tents were set up and the fire started, they poured ambergris and aloes-wood on the flames. Parviz relaxed that night and slept from the beginning of the night till dawn. When the amber jewel of the sun came out of its mine and shone the love of the day, the night died out. The great King woke up and started a joyous day.

Late afternoon, he drank a few glasses of wine. However, the wine disturbed his thought, and his heart demanded to see his love. So, he came out of his tent and mounted Shabdiz and galloped drunk toward Shirin's palace. His heart was dancing, and only a few guards from the special forces rode with him.

The news reached Shirin that King was coming toward the palace. She became frightened since they told her that he was drunk. She ordered her guards to close the gates, then also ordered them to set up a luxurious tent for the King and sent several beautiful girls with dishes full of gold coins. The tent was covered with silk and beautiful artifacts. She went to the roof and waited.

First, she saw the dust, and from it saw the light of dawn. A tall, handsome man sitting straight on his beautiful stallion appeared. Next, a figure studded with jewels with a crown on his head. His face was as beautiful as a red rosebud. He was drunk though as anyone could see from his riding.

When Shirin saw him so drunk, she froze, motionless. He was even more handsome than 13 years before and she wanted him more than ever. However, if she let him in, would he be hers or would he leave her when he became sober? That was a hard decision to make. She knew that if he left she would be miserable but what else could she do?

When the King drew close, the guards ran toward him and gave him the presents she sent. They asked him to dismount his horse and rest in the tent which was prepared for him. He ran his horse over the rugs and went toward the palace. He saw the gate locked. He neither wanted to leave nor could break the door. So, he asked one of Shirin's guards, "Go in and ask my darling, why she locked the door? What bitterness did Shirin see in me that she closed her door on me? Go and say a guest has come, what do you think—should he come in or not? Tell her, you have sweet lips why are you closing the door on your guest? Let me in since I cannot leave until I see you. If you want me to go let me see you at least."

Shirin heard what the Shah was telling the guard and started crying.

She told one of the girls, "Go and take the golden chair and set it in the tent. Then tell the King: Oh, My Lord, your nurse Shirin said that if you are my guest then do not swagger and stay where I've prepared for you. I will come to your service on the roof of the palace, and we will talk, then we will do what needs to be done."

One girl went and set up the golden chair. Another servant came in with all kinds of drinks. Then Shirin put on a purple dress and fastened it with a golden belt. She put a diadem made of pearls on her head, and with her black hair spread all over her face, she went close to the wall of the castle and bowed to the King. She threw some garnet towards Shabdiz's hooves and made the horseshoes turn red. Then she threw 100 large white pearls at Parviz's feet.

When Parviz saw her, he saw heaven sitting in a castle. But with a closed door. He jumped up and asked, "Oh, my free cyprus be fresh, healthy, and happy. The world is bright with your smile. My heart became pure with what you have done. With jewels and fine silks, you made my way beautiful, like your cradle. You pour garnet toward Shabdiz's hooves and sent me so many jewels while I was happy to see just your face. You behaved with me like honey with milk but why did you close your door? Was it my fault or yours? You left me here on the ground and went up and sat on the roof. I am not saying that I am above you, but I am your guest so why should you close the door to me? It is not right to close the door on a guest, especially the one who does not have any soul or world without you."

She said, "Oh, universally obeyed King, I hope the state will be yours forever. I hope you have the strength of an elephant and the splendor of a lion. Do not taunt me that I am sitting above you. Your slaves have room on the top. I am that dust that came from your walk. It is possible that the dust goes up. Those Kings that are watching their people have a Hindu servant on the roof. I am your guard on the roof like a Hindu.

"You said that those who are honorable would not close the door on guests. However, you are not a guest but a hunting falcon who wants the mountain dove. If you are a guest, I have given you space, and I am standing in front of you like a slave. I closed the door since you came to me while drunk. I am sitting alone here, and you are drunk, what will people say? You want to have me as a drunk and smell me like a flower then throw me away. You do not need me or my love; you are playing with me in lovemaking.

Do not hit poor Shirin with your sword. Was it not enough that you took your arrow to Rome? I have only one man to worship, and that is you, but you have more than a thousand better looking than me. If a beautiful face left you, you have ten thousand more in your castle. I am like a hen who is in the trap; its door is closed, and it is sitting on the roof. You are in your castle, and I am in this small house, your wealth is like heaven, and mine is just stone. What did you see from my love except that you are my God and my King? Did you remember, when you were drinking happily with your friends and your wife? Shah-Pour was drawing with his pen and Farhad was cutting rocks for me."

From the love he felt for her, he answered, "Oh beautiful cyprus, I want no mouth to touch yours but mine. Although your reproof has poison, it is as sweet as a sugar persecution. When you were throwing me treasure and jewelry, why did you leave me on the ground? Do not persecute me since my only guilt is my loyalty to you. Do not be so harsh; calm down. Be like a shepherd, do not be like a wolf. It is not nice to have a bad temper. That makes me ashamed.

You are both my soul and my life. If nobody else knows you know it. Either sober or drunk I did not look for anyone except your image. If anyone but I had such love in his heart, he would be disgraced. Inside I was tearing my clothing out of sadness and with difficulty made a new outfit so the army would not turn their head away from me and our Kingdom would stay intact. I was not an ordinary man to come to your house with a lute. I was a King, who could not get involved in lovemaking. However, when I would hear your name I wanted to buy it with my whole crown and throne. Although I was happy with someone else outwardly, I was in love with you with all my heart and soul. I have not done anything wrong and if I took a few steps toward success I was young then."

Shirin said, "I have so much dust in my heart for your behavior. However, your head still is full of pride for being a King. You do not need me or my love, being a King is better than having a lover. I am the bird that flew over flowers and did not see the hot summer days. In this dusty grave and stony palace, I waited for you for so long. I was like gold, refined from that heat and then became sad like ice from disappointment. There was no hand to keep me, and there was no friend to talk to. All the time I called you my love and everywhere I was loyal. However, you never did anything to let me know you even cared. Why should someone like me be so sad all the time? I am still young and beautiful. You became the heavy heart, and I became the iron soul."

Parviz said lovingly. "Do not talk to me about your beauty, since you are a hundred times more beautiful than what you say. You are the light of my eyes. If you saw your face in the mirror of my eyes, you would see a hundred times better than what you see in the mirror. If you sell your hair, I will buy it even if you sell it for a country. You are so beautiful, however, do not look at yourself since self-conceit is a sin. If you are a Queen where is the sign of your treasure? If you are sweet where is your sugar? Stop the war and let's make peace. It is customary for beautiful girls to be harsh, being nice is much better. Do not be harsh with your old lover. Why are you escaping from me like the wind from fire? Why are you throwing water at me? It is enough to run your unkind horse over me. It is enough to be harsh; it is just one night, not a year. Make me happy since I want you and came to see you."

She bowed again and said, "Oh owner of the world, the King of Kings. As long as I lived, I was in love with you. However, I did not see any love from you. You are talking about love, but it is not love but lust. Your tongue makes such a magnificent fire. You came like a flood to a pool of fish and wanted to take the fish and leave. I am going to avoid your storm; you can stay here or leave, it is up to you. I am water, the water of life. You are the fire that is the fire of youth. I do not want that water and fire mixed since all problems rise from that."

He said, "Oh the light of my eyes and my soul's candle. Please make a lover happy with your smile. You do not see your fault with that fiery temper. However, you are counting my mistakes. It is night and snow is falling like silver. Just this night let me in so I can kiss the dust of your door. You are the heaven of ripening fruits; open the gate to your heaven. Open the door and close the door to resentment. If I became disturbed, it is because you stole my consciousness. Your lips are like honey away from me, your tongue, however, stings me like a bee's bite. Do not throw a stone at Parviz's head and kill him like Farhad. You are sometimes at peace with me and other times at war. I hope God forgives you for this deceitfulness. I was searching the clouds for you like moonlight, now I found you like a cloud without water. You were like bright light, but now that I am close, you are burning like fire. From afar I saw a beautiful red flower, but now I see only the fire. When the harshness is too much, it is a war. If the ground gets hard, it is stone. Yes, I can go back and find someone better than you. However, I am trying to have the happiness we felt when we were young."

She said, "Oh King of good fortune, both your crown and your throne are beautiful on you. You are the great King, who can defeat the world's strongest heroes. I hope your luck stays with you since you are the sunshine of this land."

Then she became harsh like a mountain of fire and said, "Oh great King you are a true King. Go since lovemaking is a symbolic ceremony for Kings. The lovers are those who have only one lover. Do not taunt me with Farhad's love; you should remember a person who is gone with respect. For me, Farhad with his kindness was a brother. He never got anything from me or heard my song.

Although I made his life bitter like bitter aloes-wood, his anguish was sweet. I saw thousands of displays of compassionate modesty from him but did not hear even one message from you one day.

"For me, a thorn that has a flower is better than a cyprus that never bears fruit. The lover is like a sea of stone; I am like a mountain. That stone is hitting my head. I am in prison like an iron inside the stone; my heart is without joy and any friend. Think that one morning there was a fast wind which took a leaf from your orchard. The flood of sadness made me wonder. You get on your horse and go back. That story that you heard about me is gone, and my kindnesses that you saw are in the past. I swear that although you are our King, without marriage, you cannot reach me." She turned away and left the roof.

CHAPTER 44

Returning to His Camp

In the night, with the drops of snow and rain pouring down, the King headed back. Shabdiz looked gray with the snow all around her. The King was buried in his thought. He had tried to get her to change her mind, but nothing worked. The harder he played the trumpet, the harsher was her answer.

When he reached the campground, he was in despair; his heart was burning. He could not sleep. He asked all his advisors and ministers to leave, and he was alone with Shah-Pour.

That master painter tried to cheer him up. He told him, "Shirin is kind, do not mind her sharp tongue. Do not mind poor Shirin, who is fiery; you know that it is told that sweet things are also hot."

Parviz said miserably, "You do not know what happened today and what she did to me. She was so furious; she was a woman without fear or shame. I put down my hat and apologized, however, neither the cold weather made her kinder, nor her fiery temper calmed down. Her tongue was like an arrow and an ax. Yes, friends sometimes get mad at each other, but they don't act like thorn against a thorn.

"Although being away from her now makes me sad. I know

how to take care of it. It seems that she is against me although she pretends that she loves me. As much I demanded her kindness she did not accept anything. Although her love is so sweet and there is no one as sweet as her in the world, it is not worth my pride and dignity."

Shah-Pour bowed and said, "My greatest Majesty, you cannot get angry at her harshness. With your generosity forgive her. A lover's fight is like thunder. There is little difference between fear and coquetry. Although you are mad at Shirin, you cannot forget her love, but you may have to accept her mincing air. All good-looking women are a bit harsh. Have you seen any flower without thorns? From old times, the beauties were unmanageable. However, they are like a water snake whose stinks are meek. If you want to get rid of your sadness, you should stay put like a mountain. How do you know that she is not miserable herself? I know she is madly in love with you, but she is patient. If there is a stone falling, it will hit only your shadow, but it will hit her head. If there are thorns of fear, they will tear your skirt, but they will rip her heart. Do not be mad at that moon since she is a woman and cannot take a risk. When she was very young and inexperienced, she jumped to see you. In your court, she was exposed to all manners of jealousy from the women of the court. From then on, she decided to be with you as your only love and wife, not the slave of your lust for just a few days."

Parviz interrupted him and said, "What do you think I was doing today? I went there to be with her and make her my Queen. But she refused me! The King of the Persian Empire! She should know that I can have any woman I want but went there, and I wanted only her."

Shah-Pour bowed again and said "Your Majesty have you told her your intention? Did you ask her to marry you?"

Husrō-Parviz frowned and said, "Not in that manner. But I

wrote her a letter to come to me, and she refused. I went to see her myself and told her how much I loved her. I told her that all these 13 years away from her I did not forget her even one minute. Does not she know when a King goes to her what it means?"

"Oh, my Royal Highness, you know, when we have a wild horse who is unmanageable, we start slow. We show patience, and gradually we can put anything on its shoulders. With patience, the prisoners become free. Patience is the key to any locked job. Usually, when the rope gets tight and challenging, you open it. The dawn laughs when the night gets too dark. I am sure your sadness will be changed to happiness, and you will find what you want." He hoped his words would calm the King and make him hopeful and happy.

CHAPTER 45

⁓⁓⁓

The Wedding

When the Shah left, Shirin stoned her heart for being so harsh on him. She was crying and could not stop her tears from pouring out. She could not stop her sadness nor stop her heart from demanding to see her King. She was so disturbed by her internal turmoil she became ashamed of what she had done to the King.

She mounted Golgoon. The horse was red and her face was too. She rode swiftly on the back of that beautiful horse. The road was narrow and as dark as her hair. She was wearing the guard's clothing and went after Shah-Hanshah's Shabdiz. All the way her tears poured out. She rode hard until she got to Parviz's campground. She saw that the guard's tongue was silent, and no colonel was on the site. The opium of moonlight infected all of them, and all lay down drunk with sleep. She looked around and did not know what to do next.

After the King had fallen asleep, Shah-Pour left the tent. He saw a figure riding fast towards the camp. He went towards the figure without waking up any of the guards. When the horse pulled to a halt before him, Shah-Pour asked, "Oh which kind of delicate man are you? Are you a fairy? If you are not fairy why are you here? You should know that if the lion gets here, you will have no power. Even snakes become as small as ants here."

Shirin heard his voice and recognized him, so she dismounted the horse. Shah-Pour, who was wondering why she jumped down from her horse, went closer to see who it was. It was then that he recognized her. He dropped his hat, bowed and said, "What happened that you came? You know that the dust of you shines like pearls in my eyes."

She said, "Oh, dear Shah-Pour, thank God it is you." Then she held his hand and said, "Let's go somewhere where I can tell you my story. I was so harsh with the King of my heart, and I am so ashamed of myself. I said things without thinking just like the rooster singing at the wrong time. After he left, I was so sad and embarrassed that I did not know what to do. I decided to follow him. I am so happy that you saw me and nobody else did."

Shah-Pour said with respect, "Now, what do you want to do My Lady?"

"I have two demands and want you to take care of them for me."

"Please tell me what you want Your Majesty, I will try what I can."

"I want to sit in the corner and see my King from a distance. I want to see his handsome face and his joy."

"Oh, Your Highness I will obey your command. There are two tents for the King. One is for his drinking and the other for sleeping. He was not feeling good and was talking to me until late, and he fell asleep in the drinking tent. I will take you to his sleeping tent." Then he fastened Golgoon in the stable next to Shabdiz and took Shirin to the tent next to where Parviz was sleeping. He then returned to the King. He lit a candle, and the Shah woke up.

His face showed excitement, "My dear friend, I was sleeping, but you were awake sitting by me! You are a dear friend. I dreamed that I was so happy, and I was flying up to the sky. I dreamed that I was in a big orchard where I found a dazzling light. Can you interpret my dream, please?"

"My Highness, be healthy and dominant all the time. I would say that your eyes will be bright from that bright light. God will end this sadness of yours, your dark night will change to daylight, and you will find that beautiful lady of yours. So, for good fortune let's take the dust of the night and be calm. Tomorrow, please have a party and drink wine. When from the past comes the spring of light, we will be happy and wait for your good luck."

The King was so happy when he heard the interpretation of his dream he fell to sleep again. The next morning, he woke up happy from the dreams of the previous night. He let the day start with the customary ceremony. He was sitting on a throne in a sixty by sixty tent. Everyone stood. The royal colonels stood by the door like golden figures. On their back, the black from Habasheh and Turks from China showed like the moon visiting the night.

The usual visiting hours passed and all the colonels left with his permission, and only a few friends stayed back. His two musicians and his closest friends were present. All over, dishes were designed with rubies and emeralds. Cupbearers and servants were passing drinks and fruit to the audiences. Barbed was holding his barbath (a musical instrument like lyre) and with his hands made beautiful notes that would cure any injury of the heart. From the smoke of his heart, he would fire the lyre; the barbath would yell like David. The sound of music from his instrument had the same magical cure as Jesus's breath. When he started his music, even birds would fall asleep in ecstasy.

Nakisa was the name of Parviz's harp player. No one could play and sing like him. His music was so good that the birds would dive to the ground. Except for him, nobody could compete with Barbed. That afternoon both of them started playing. The sound of their music was mixed with the aroma of perfume mixed with a beautiful rainbow color. They played for hours, then Parviz permitted them to leave, and he went for a short ride before his nightly party.

Shah-Pour went to see Shirin, and she asked him, "Please send one of those musicians to me. I want him to play like my wounded heart and tell whatever I wish to say to my love."

Shah-Pour took Nakisa to her tent and asked him to make a song according to Shirin's specification. Then he asked Barbed to make a song answering Nakisa.

When daylight gave up and the night spread its black tent over the universe, King Parviz sat down to listen to his musicians. Nakisa started to play and sang: "I hope my luck does not sleep and give me a glimpse of hope. Oh, the morning of hope, please come out of the mountain of the patient and make my heart as light as the sunshine. Oh, my luck for just a few days be kind to me and get a key to open my prison and defeat the army of sorrow. I do not claim to be a King but your slave. I am a helpless and disabled stranger who is so sad. I am like that flower who tears her petals for her love, like that tulip who becomes old in her youth. I lost my world just for a slim hope. I have no friend to keep me warm with his love. My heart is lonely."

Barbed started his note and sang: "Oh the breeze brings the aroma of my friend. My light sees the image of treasure. Which water is coming from this waterway? Which wind has such a magnificent aroma? Did the moon come inside the porthole that the night became bright? Is it possible that the wind of heaven passed by us that we are so happy? Did our luck light a new candle that burned the wing of sadness like the wing of a butterfly? Did Shirin spread her sweet lips so I could hear her calling from everywhere? Tell that fairy to bring us good luck. Do not pay attention to my anger, look at my curtsy and see how I became tame. Let me get close to you; it is not nice to give a thorn instead of a flower."

Nakisa answered: "Oh I will be so happy to see you; your home is much better for me than a rose garden. Your face gives light to the stars, and the world concedes your kindness. What are you drinking that your face is as beautiful as spring flowers? If you take a mirror and look into it, you will become drunk with love of yourself. However, you do not need any mirror since you have my eyes that see no face but yours. I swear to God, who has all the world in his power that my sweet life is like poison without you. Since I cannot be close to you, at least, let me see you from a distance. It will be such a glorious day that I can hold you in my arms and have you give me wine. I keep your hair in the middle of the night and die in front of you at dawn. Oh, I do not have a tolerance for being away from you. I'd rather be killed in front of you than be alive without you."

Barbed sang: "Yesterday I got drunk and passed the door of an orchard. In that orchard, I saw spring. There were a hundred petals of flowers with a thorn on each petal. There was a treasure that was held prisoner inside the castle's fence. Inside the wall, there was a beautiful woman who closed the door on me. That fairy face who has a house in my heart has made my heart crazy. While I am awake, my brain is so sad since that fairy does not get away from my mind. If I sleep, she pushes my brain and makes me mad in sleep. My angry heart wants that fairy in the palace, not in ruins. If that treasure comes out of her ruins, I will give her a crown inlaid with pure pearls. I swear to those magical eyes, and that smoky hair of hers that fills me with fire. Swear to those drunken eyes whose reproof afflicted me but told me to stay put. If she comes to me, she will be my soul as long as I am alive. I may be King of the world but will be her slave. Oh, my idol vixen please forgive me, if I did not do what you wanted I tasted the poison of regret. Let's say whatever I did, was a sin, aren't my tears apologizing? I am remorseful for whatever I did; my witness is my lack of sleep. My share of life was a hello from you, and in that too you closed the door. I do not have any hope that you'd ask how I am. If my name comes to your mind, that is enough. Your heart does not want to come to me. I do not have that luck."

When Shirin heard Barbed's song, she cried out loud. Parviz heard the cry and stopped the musicians, dismissed everyone and jumped up to go toward the noise. Shah-Pour grabbed his hand and said, "Please stay put."

Although Parviz was disturbed, he sat down. "What was this heartbreaking cry? Find it out for me." Before Shah-Pour could answer the King, a fairy figure came out of the tent like the moon coming out of clouds and, as a drunken woman fell at the King's feet. When the King saw his sweetheart, he bent down and grabbed both of her arms. He pulled her up and held her in his arms and started kissing her. He told her he wanted to gather all his prominent people and marry her. She looked at him and was so overjoyed she could say nothing.

They were happy together looking into each other's eyes and saying how miserable they were all those 13 years they were apart.

A week later Parviz sent Shirin back to her palace with a group of his army. He then went to his capital. He asked the astronomers to find a good day for his wedding. The King started the party for his bride with a thousand young camels with red hair and yellow dots, a thousand horses, and many chests full of jewelry. Many men and women wearing their best clothing went to Shirin's palace and brought her to the capital city.

Every step she took, he had coins poured on her feet until she got to his palace. Parviz sat next to Shirin and the Mobed married them. That night they stayed up all night and day, then they slept the next day and night.

For one month, they had their honeymoon then he started his duties again as a King. He decided to gift his friends with the joy he felt. Farangis married Shah-Pour. Homila married Nakisa, and Saman-khatoon married Barbed. Then Parviz gave Armenia to Shah-Pour, and he became the Shah of Armenian. After that, Parviz's life was full of joy. Being young, with his lover by his side and ruling the Kingdom—what else could he want?

CHAPTER 46

Shirin Gives Parviz a Child

It was the spring of 604 AD, in the court of Shah-Hanshah Parviz, the Empire of Greater Persia. The heads of the army, the ministers, the chairman of the states and foreign consular all were waiting in the majestic hall of the palace. Those in the lobby were amused by the dazzling luxury of the place. The silk curtain studded with gems was hanging at the end of the hall. The beautiful 27 by 50 meter rug woven of silk, gold and silver thread on the floor dazzled the eyes of all who saw it. The rug was a painting of the Garden of Eden, with rivers and waterfalls as natural as can be. The tree trunks were made of silver. Their leaves were made of light green silk while their blossoms were made of brightly colored silks. Their fruits were made of green emeralds, red rubies, sapphire, topaz, and pearl. The ground was woven from golden thread. It seemed that the waterfalls glittered with what appeared to be diamonds.

Everyone was waiting for the appearance of the King of Kings, Shah-Hanshah Parviz. They all knew that the meeting would be much shorter since Queen Shirin was in labor and the Shah-Hanshah needed to be with her as soon as possible. The crowd's excitement rose high when the announcer said, "Long live the

King of Kings." The silk curtain opened up, and the young King's face appeared. He was again sitting on his golden throne wearing a silk tunic covered with gems, a pink vest with many pearls sewed on its edges and his pleated pants fastened to his ankles by a thin thread. As always, the most dazzling was his crown adorned with jewels of ruby, emerald, and pearl. The crown was made of gold and since it was too heavy to wear the King would sit under it before the curtain opened up. It hung from the ceiling by a golden chain which was not visible from a distance. The Great Mobed started his prayer, "In the name of Ahura Mazda. I pray for His Majesty's well-being and that the Prince to be born healthy and His Majesty add more lands to his Empire."

Then each audience member started reporting their findings. The foreign consulares gave the King their messages and offered their gifts. Soon the gathering was done, and everyone but his advisors left the hall.

King Parviz came down from his throne and started pacing the room. No one dared to say a thing. The minutes passed very slowly, and there was no news from inside the palace. It was a long labor which worried all the gathering including the young King. But as it is, time passes even if it is long and hard and finally a maid came in with a broad smile. She bowed and said, "Long live the King and the newborn Prince who just arrived. He is a healthy and beautiful child."

King Parviz said, "Thank you for the good news, I'd like to see my son as soon as possible." He gave a gold coin to the maid.

The girl bowed again and said, "Long live the King, Queen, and newborn Prince. He is getting dressed. You will be able to visit him and his mother anytime you wish."

The audience called, "Congratulations, and long live the King and newborn Prince."

King Parviz said, "Thank you, I am going to see my son but call the astronomer to come and read his fortune."

The prime minister said. "I've heard it and will obey."

The King went to see his son and Queen Shirin his first and only love. He had many children, so his worry was not for his newborn son but his love, Shirin.

The room was covered with silk carpet knotted with rosettes so small only children could make them. The vessels for flowers and libations were all made of silver. The cushions and the bedspread sparked, for they were woven with silver thread. The Queen was laid in there wore thick gold armbands with hanging torques and pearls and the same combination of stones on her forehead.

However, the Queen looked like a beautiful flower even without all the jewelry and the silk clothing. She rose from her bed to welcome her husband. But the King signaled her not to move and rushed to her bedside.

He bent down and kissed her lips and said, "I am so happy that you are okay. I was so worried about you. You went through so much pain for so long!"

The Queen smiled and said, "Long live my King. All the pain in the world is bearable when I see your smile and hold our son in my arms."

The King brushed the hair from her forehead. The nanny brought in the child. He was washed and wrapped in a beautiful silk garment. King Parviz held him in his arms and said, "Oh, he is so handsome."

"Yes, he is, he looks like you," said the Queen.

"How do you know? He is just born, and usually, you cannot tell who a newborn looks like." The King smiled down at his son with affection and love.

"I know since you are the most handsome man I've seen in

my life, and I see the resemblance on his face even now," said the Queen.

"Well, I think if he should resemble one of us it should be you who is the most beautiful creature in the universe. What should we name him?"

"MardanShah is a lovely name if you agree."

The King bent down and kissed Shirin with the passion of a man in love and said, "That's it then. MardanShah."

Once again Parviz attended a ceremony for his son. The ceremony was done in Atashkedeh, the fire temple located in the palace. The high priest, Mobed Mobdedan, and several high-ranking priests attended the ceremony. The temple was a simple round room with several rectangular rooms around it. In the middle of the round room was the flame of divine fire. Around the fire stood eight men with white robes and white hats. They too were Mobeds.

Shah-Hanshah arrived, and everyone bowed in respect. He sat on his throne which had been brought into the temple for him. The Mobeds started chanting the Gathas, the sacred songs of Zarathustra.

The chanting finished, and the high priest prayed for the King's victory and good health. He got up and took a tomar, a rolled animal skin that was used as paper, to the King. He stood in front of the King, bowed and said, "Your Majesty this is the forecast of your son's future life. Keep it in a safe place, and it should not be opened until his death arrives. I cannot tell you what his life will be like. But I am glad to inform you that he will bring luck to you, and the Persian Empire will expand to be as wide as Achaemene's Empire.

King Parviz put it in the box that was prepared for this event, and they sealed the box. He was happy that there was no warning or bad news about his newborn son. They did not mention his

Kingdom but said he would bring a good fortune to him and his country.

Parviz thought, *He already had brought me happiness; he and his mother are my greatest fortunes.*

CHAPTER 47

Problems at Home

There was one problem in Parviz's life, and that was Shiruya, his first son by Maryam. It is legend that when Parviz married Shirin, Shiruya was eleven years old and was telling everyone that Shirin should have been his wife instead. The King was upset with his son.

One day he said to Bozorg-Mehr, "My wise man, I am heavy-hearted from this son of mine. I am afraid of how bad his future will be. Because of his evil thoughts, his mother is not safe with him. I do not see any good coming out of him since he is the child of fire and ashes. He does not say anything accepted by the people; he says what he likes to say. I do not see any lordship in his behavior. He is like smoke coming from my fire. He is my son but is farthest from me. I have taken the crown from so many Kings but if I have a son like him what is the use? He is neither kind with Shirin nor with me. I might as well be a snake to have such a son. Not all flowers bear fruit. So many children kill their parents like iron which breaks the stone. There are so many who are not relatives but are more loyal than one's own family."

Bozorg-Mehr said, "My King, your pure heart knows good from bad. I assume that this son gives you a headache; is not he your son? It is not possible to be your child's enemy and empty your heart of the relationship. You are good, and your child cannot be evil. Usually, the plants come out from the seed we sow. If this son of yours is unmanageable, be happy since time will change him. Right now, he is young. When he grows older, he will forget his harshness."

When Shiruya was sixteen years old, he was as tall as a thirty year old. The King brought wise nobles to teach his son. Mobed was watching him per the King's instruction, but he did not see him eager to learn. He always wanted to play rather than be taught. One day, he went to him and saw that his book was in front of him, but the monstrous young man had in his left hand a dried wolf claw, in his right hand he had a buffalo horn. He was hitting buffalo horn to the wolf claw and vice versa. Mobed was saddend by his useless play. He felt very disturbed seeing the bad omen of the wolf claw since he knew about the astronomers' findings for the boy's future. The news was relayed, and the King was made aware of it. Parviz's face became pale and sadness crept over him. The agony he felt when he heard the astrologer after his son's birth came rushing back, and he wondered what could be done. However, he still could not hurt his own son on the word of an astrologer, so he tried to overcome his fear and sadness.

It was this way was until Shiruya turned twenty and claimed that he should be King. Parviz was very sad and put him under house arrest. Shiruya and his friends lived in a large palace with beautiful gardens. All types of food and clothes, wine and musicians were sent to this palace so the Prince would not be lonely or bored. There were also forty men sent to guard the palace.

CHAPTER 48

The King's Murder

Parviz was victorious and loved by everyone until he became ill and was eventually defeated by the Roman army. Sick and weak, he announced that his son MardanShah would be his Crown Prince. This announcement was not welcomed by his generals or the Persian nobles. They were tired of constant war with the Byzantines, and some joined with Heraclius, who wanted peace. They decided that Parviz's first born son should be the King, not MardanShah, his son with Shirin, so they joined with Parviz's first son Qobād, nicknamed Shiruya a. Now, Parviz was put under house arrest, and only Shirin was permitted to be with him. Parviz was so happy to be with Shirin that even with a chain on his feet he said, "I am free." He told his moon. "Do not worry, because it is destiny. Whenever there is a fire, it usually sends its smoke towards the good people. The hunter's arrow will reach the most beautiful prey. However, I do not care about my throne. Since you are with me I still feel like I am a King."

Shirin also comforted him and said, "In ruling a country, this kind of thing happens. Sometimes there is happiness and sometimes sickness. If we let the sadness overcome us, we will be dead.

We should not let that happen since we cannot be imprisoned with both our minds and our bodies. The terminally ill person can come back from certain death while a healthy person can become ill. Not everyone who has a fever will die. You are a wise man, just do not be sad since the sadness will bring more pain. If the devil took your throne, I am sure he will get his punishment. In this country, people turn their heads from good. We are forced to tolerate anything. You cannot fight with destiny. There are two people destiny cannot touch: the dead and the unborn. Nobody stays alive forever. If the world were stable, then there would never be a new King. Now that you are in prison, do not get upset since you are a treasure and the treasure is always hidden. Do not see yourself as small since you are the heart of the world. Think that God has chosen you and made the world for you and you will become happy and not care about your throne or your Kingdom. If you need them, think that the earth is your throne, and the sun is your crown." She tried to make him happy all day until the night's wings fell over the world.

It was a dark night that stole the light from the moon. The King's feet were in a golden chain, and Shirin put her legs on his legs and told him sweet stories so he would become calm and fall asleep. When finally, Parviz fell asleep Shirin fell asleep too.

The world says that trouble arrives drunk. From the door, came a devilish face who did not have any love in his heart. Like a thief who tries to find valuable things, he searched for the King. He came to his bed and stabbed him through his chest so that the blood jumped out like light from the cloud. When he had separated the sun from the moon, he left the prison.

The King woke up in pain. The room was full of his blood, and he was thirsty. He wanted to wake Shirin and ask her to get him some water. But he decided against it. He thought, *If she wakes up now and sees me like this, she will not sleep anymore and will cry until morning. It is better if I do not say anything and die while she is sleeping.*

That loyal lover gave up his soul and did not wake up Shirin. The feel of the warm blood running from the King's body eventually roused Shirin awake though. She became anxious like a bird seeing a trap. The treasury was empty, and the army was gone, and the commander-in-chief was dead. She searched for the sunshine in the night but only saw dark ruins.

She cried for several hours which made the night darker. Then she decided to move. She mixed rose water with ambergris and poured them on the bloody body. She washed him with rose water and camphor until it became as clean as the light.

CHAPTER 49

Shirin and the New King

With his father dead, Qobād (Shiruya) wanted his stepmother more than ever. The love he felt as a teenager was still burning him inside. However, he did not mention it to anybody. After Parviz had been killed, he sent someone to Shirin to tell her, "Please be happy and do not mourn my father's death. As soon as a week and two months pass, you will be a flower in my orchard. I will give you all the power you desire and give you more glory than what Parviz gave you. I will keep you like a treasure and give you the key to my treasure."

When Shirin heard these words, she became sour like vinegar. She told her companion, "How stupid is he that he does not know that I do not wish to see him either at the funeral or a wedding. He killed my sons and my dear husband and now he wants me to be his wife!"

She decided to deceive him and said, "I am not without any need from my King. Give me my property and let me do what I want with it and wait until we bury the late King."

Qobād believed her. He let her take anything she wanted from the court. So, she took everything that belonged to her and *Husrō-Parviz* then gave it to the poor and needy. She also gave some to the fire temple.

CHAPTER 50

Shirin's Last Day

The next day, as soon as dawn woke up from its nightly sleep, Shirin ordered her servants to prepare a litter from aloes-wood covered with pearl and gold. According to the Persian religion, she lay down Parviz in that Cradle. Early in the morning some of Parviz's nobles put the cradle on their shoulders and marched toward the tomb which was prepared for him. All the nobles were walking by foot around the otherworldly bed. Barbed, who cut his finger to show his sorrow was there, and so was Bozorg-Omid (a minister of the court), who was scared and trembling like a branch of the willow tree. He cried out, "Oh the loss of the King's life is so hard for us. Where is the protector of the Persian Kings? Where is the commander-in-chief, his sword, and his flag?"

The servant's men and women all had their hair open, and between them, Shirin was walking tall. She wore jeweled earrings and spread her hair on her shoulders. She had a yellow silk scarf like the sun on her head and wore a red dress like Venus. She was merrily following the King's cradle, dancing. All the way, that moon was dancing until they got to the dome of the King. Behind her, all the servants were crying. People who saw Shirin acting this way did not think she was sorry for her husband's assassination. Qobād was assured that Shirin must like him and his proposal.

They put the bed in the tomb and stood in front of it. The Mobed sang the usual prayer then Shirin said she wanted to say goodbye to her slain husband, and all left the tomb except Shirin.

She closed the tomb and went toward Parviz's body with a poniard in her hand. She opened the King's clothing and kissed the scar that killed him; then she hit the same place in her chest with the dagger. She hugged his body and put her lips on his. Then she cried out, "My soul is joined with the soul and body of my love."

It had been a long time since Shirin had entered the tomb, so one of the men waiting outside decided to ask her to come out so they could close the door. When he went in, he saw her dead body.

When the news reached the new King, he was devastated and became ill. He ordered a new tomb for her and buried her there.

We still can see through the dust of the crumbled buildings, Shirin's picture on the cave that Farhad dug, her ruined castle, and the waterway. So the legend of three people, and three love affairs lives on and is still the sweetest love story for young Persians.

The poet ended his story, and we come back to present time. Such an amazing story but how much of it was true? It seemed that luck did not only turn away from Parviz and Shirin, but it turned its back on all of Persia. Only seven months later, Qobād (Shiruya) died of the plague that took over the Persian Empire and killed more than half of the population. The bad omen was carried not only by the plaque but the beginning invasion of the Persian Empire by Arab conquerors five years after Parviz's murder. We must turn to historians to tell us why Parviz was killed and what truly happened to the Persian Empire.

CHAPTER 51

History: The Wish Comes True but Does It Last?

In 608 the Sasanian armies invaded and plundered Syria and Asia Minor. They then began an advance that would eventually reach Chalcedon. Parviz was eager to expand his Empire without thinking of the consequences it would bring. He was not aware of the danger in his own court, the divisiveness within his army due to religious differences. He was a King with a Queen he loved and worshiped. Was his giving Armenia to Rome, and then taking it back, the right decision? History would be the judge. He refused to look back and question if his actions were mistakes.

Parviz's relationship with Christianity was complicated; his wife Maryam and his children were Christian. During his reign, there was a constant conflict between Monophysite and Nestorian Christians. Parviz favored the Monophysites and ordered all his subjects to adhere to Monophysitism, perhaps under the influence of his royal physician Gabriel of Sinjar, who supported that faith. Parviz also dispensed money and gifts to the Christian shrines. Parviz's high tolerance for Christianity and friendship with the

Christian Byzantines made some Armenian writers think that Parviz was himself a Christian. His positive policy toward the religion, although politically motivated, caused Christianity to significantly spread around the Sasanian Empire. This made him unpopular with the Zoroastrian priests. When Zoroastrians criticized him, he would repeat his father's words, "The throne and the government can only be safe if it gains the goodwill of both religions."

In 610, Heraclius, an Armenian, revolted against Phocas in Rome and killed him, crowning himself emperor of the Byzantine. He then tried to negotiate peace with Parviz by sending diplomats to his court. Parviz, however, rejected their offer. His ex-brother-in-law wanted to control the Byzantine Empire and Parviz dreamed of a rule that spanned both Empires. He decided it would be best if his brother-in-law became the emperor of the Byzantine instead.

This became one of his worst mistakes. Heraclius was Armenian and Christian, and so were most of the people in the Persian Armenian territory. Their loyalty was first to their religion, and second to the Persian Empire. He also set a good example for the Persian generals who wanted more power. If Heraclius could do it, so could they.

At the time, Parviz was still young and mighty. His generals were adding new territory to his Kingdom. He had no need to accept the new Roman Empire's peace offer. Damascus and Jerusalem were captured in 613 and 614, by his General Shahrbaraz and the True Cross was carried away in triumph. Another Persian general called Shahin occupied Egypt in 618. This victory fulfilled another of *Husrō*-Parviz goals: to extend his territory back to the size of Persian Empire in the time of Achaemenids.

There is a Persian proverb that says, *When the fountain goes up eventually it will fall.* Parviz was fifty-four when two of his generals, Farrukh Hormozd, and his son Rostam Farrokhzad, rebelled against him. They welcomed Heraclius into northern Atropatene in 624. Heraclius then began sacking cities and temples, including the Adur Gushnasp temple.

In 627, Heraclius defeated the Persian army at the Battle of Nineveh and advanced towards Tisfoon (Ctesiphon). Parviz, who was 58 and suffered from diarrhea, fled from his favorite residence, Dastagird (near Ctesiphon), without resisting.

He again rejected the peace treaty with Heraclius, who in return captured Dastagird and plundered it. The sickness took Parviz's sharpness and bravery from him, and his letter to general Shahrbaraz was intercepted so he did not receive the help he was expecting.

The feuding families included; Shahrbaraz, who represented the Mihran family; the house of Ispahbudhan represented by spahbed Farrukh Hormizd and his two sons Rostam Farrokhzad and Farrukhzad (sitting governors of Azerbaijan and Kurdistan); the Armenian faction represented by Varaztirots II Bagratuni; and finally, the Kanarang (the governor of Khorasan). It was these groups who decided to overthrow the King.

In February, Qobād, along with Aspad Gushnasp, captured Tisfoon and imprisoned Parviz. Qobād II then proclaimed himself as King of the Sasanian Empire on 25 February, and with the aid of Piruz Parviz, executed all his brothers and half-brothers, including Parviz's favorite son MardanShah.

Historians say Parviz "exceeded most of the other Persian Kings in bravery, wisdom, and forethought, and none matched him in military might and triumph, or hoarding of treasures and good fortunes. Hence the epithet Parviz, meaning victorious. When he was the King of Persia, he emulated the feats of the Achaemenids. He conquered the rich Roman provinces of the Middle East."[1] Aside from his love story, much literature has been written about him which blames his actions for the fall of the Persian Empire 20 years after his assassination.

Some blame him for his pride which caused him to be at war most of his life. Although conquering new lands made him the most powerful emperor in the history of his time, people grew tired of constant war, which caused dissatisfaction in his support. Therefore, his generals freed his imprisoned son Qobād and killed Parviz. This account can be considered true, but the family reasons of greed, covetousness, and jealousy are absent.

Almost all those who overthrew Parviz had some relation with the Roman Empire at some point in their lives. That is why, after killing Parviz, Kavadh(Shiruya) then made peace with the Byzantine emperor Heraclius and gave the Byzantines all their lost territories, their captured soldiers, a war indemnity, the True Cross, and other relics lost in Jerusalem in 614.

These generals wanted power, and they did not care what would happen to their country. Without understanding that greed was their motive, we cannot comprehend why, before they killed the King (*Husrō*-Parviz) they killed his 15 sons. They wanted no Prince to claim the throne but one who blindly obeyed them.

Unfortunately, none of those nobles could make the others agree to his rule, and an internal war followed further weakened the Empire and tore the country. There are some stories about Parviz being superstitious and acted according to the astrologers' findings. Therefore, they blame him for the Empire's collapse.

Recall the following were foretold:

In the convent, the priest told Parviz that he would become a King and stay on the throne for 38 years and his uncle was going to hurt him but would be killed by him. Later his uncle rebelled against him, and Parviz's order saw him murdered.

The astronomer told Parviz that his son was a bad omen. When his son became 20, Parviz put him under house arrest. The same son eventually had him killed along with each of his 15 children.

Parviz was told that he would be murdered by a man from the east. He shot a man thinking he was the one foretold but he was wrong. The slain man's son was the one hired by Qobād to kill Parviz.

He was told that one of his grandchildren would cause the Persian Empire to collapse. His grandson was the last Sassanid King. He was defeated by the Arabs and was killed.

He was told an Arab would invade his country. In 600, Parviz executed Al-Nu'man III, King of the Lakhmids of Al-Hira. He thought he was the one that astronomers had warned him about. But his action made the border unsafe, and later the Arabs easily attacked Iran.

If we believe the above claims as true, we have to admit that the people in those times could predict life's events precisely, which is hard to believe.

What happened to those who conspired against Parviz? All of them but two lost their lives within five years of his assassination.

The Ispahbudhan spahbed Farrukh Hormizd was killed by Siyavakhsh in a palace plot on the orders of Azarmidokht (Parviz's daughter who became Shah-Hanshah) after he proposed to her in an attempt to usurp the Sasanian throne.

Rostam Farrokhzad was killed when fighting the Arabs. Shahrbaraz seized the throne from Ardashir III (Qobād 's son) and was killed by Sasanian nobles after forty days.

The fate of the Persian and Roman Empires were not that different from the fates of the conspirators. Both Empires fought and weakened each other to the point that the new Muslims from Arabia were able to destroy one, weaken the other, and build an Islamic Empire from their ashes.

GLOSSARY

Gathas	Zoroastrian prayer hymns
gaur	zebra-like mammal
Husrō	King
Javidan	a Persian word meaning "live forever"
kamancheh	bowed string instrument
kasra	Persian word commonly associated with "the leader"
Kelileh va Demneh	also known as Panchatantra, Indian work of political philosophy
Mobed	Zoroastrian priest
Monophysite	believers that Jesus Christ is only of one nature and not two
Nestorian	believers seeing Jesus as both human and divine in nature
Nowruz	Persian new year
shabrang	black or the color of night
Shah	a man or a woman who rules a country or a region, King or Queen
Shah-Hanshah	the King of Kings
Shahrood	a river in Armenia
Shahnameh	epic poem about the history of Iran
spahbed	army chief
tomar	a rolled animal skin that was used as paper
Zand	Zoroastrian translations and commentary on texts

REFERENCES

1. Revolvy. "Muhammad ibn Jarir al-Tabari." Revolvy.com. https://www.revolvy.com/main/index.php?s=Muhammad+ibn+Jarir+al-Tabari .

2. Nizami, Ganjavi. "Khosrow and Shirin." Persia, ca. 1193

3. Ferdowsi. "The Shahnameh." Persia, ca. 1010

ABOUT THE AUTHOR

Maryam has been writing and publishing stories and poems in her native Persian for more than 20 years. She earned her masters from Shiraz University and moved to the U.S., where she attended graduate school at SUNY Binghamton School of Advanced Technology. She has four published books which you can find listed on the next page.

Other Books by This Author

We Really Appreciate You Reading This Book!

Friend Maryam on Facebook:
https://www.facebook.com/mtabibzaeh
or https://www.facebook.com/maryam.tabibzadeh.3
or https://www.facebook.com/Danger-o
f-Love-1484903665057255/
or https://www.facebook.com/search/
top/?q=Danger%20Of%20LOve

Favorite her Smashwords author page: https://www.
smashwords.com/profile/view/Maryamtabibadeh

Connect on LinkedIn:
https://www.linkedin.com/in/
maryam-tabibzadeh-4450b37?trk=hp-identity-name

Visit her website:
http://www.Persiandreams.org

www.ingramcontent.com/pod-product-compliance
Lightning Source LLC
Chambersburg PA
CBHW050358030726
47503CB00006B/1908